Books are to b~
~

French for Kissing

+++

Sophie Parkin's main ambition in life is to have as much fun as humanly possible. This has manifested itself in many ways throughout the years. As a rug rat it was making mud and worm pies, and as she got older she maintained her interest in cooking but added chatting and climbing trees to her array of abilities as a seasoned tomboy.

Sophie has a degree in Fine Art, otherwise known as painting, chatting, writing, partying, chatting and having fun, and the occasional chat. She often thought about marrying her phone, but then e-mail was invented, and mobiles. In between chatting, she has had two children (Paris and Carson, who are great chatterers), has had painting exhibitions, run nightclubs, written grown-up novels and for newspapers, been a kids' Agony Aunt for AOL and cooked quite a lot. She has no pets or husbands as she is allergic to both – except for a stray cat called Cat, who loves her only for her copious gifts of milk and salmon. It is a simple one-way relationship.

This is her first teenage novel. Unlike Lily, Sophie has never passed a French exam, and has never learned to speak another language, however she does love Paris (her son and the city) and is very fond of berets and most French food that doesn't involve cow, sheep or pigs' intestines.

.

French for Kissing

Sophie Parkin

Piccadilly Press • London

For Carson, a beautiful Sunflower amongst the Lilys

First published in Great Britain in 2005
by Piccadilly Press Ltd,
5 Castle Road, London NW1 8PR
www.piccadillypress.co.uk

A catalogue record for this book is available from the British Library

ISBN: 1 85340 891 3 (trade paperback)

1 3 5 7 9 10 8 6 4 2

Printed and bound in Great Britain by Bookmarque Ltd
Text design by Textype, Cambridge
Cover design by Susan Hellard and Fielding Design
Set in ITC Legacy

CHAPTER ONE

Vegetable, Mineral or Animal?

As if my name isn't bad enough – Lily Lovitt, and before you ask I am NOT lovin' it – my family is even more embarrassing than my name. My mum thinks she's really witty, and a Prince Charles in the garden. It is not unusual for her to say, 'I'm spiritually connected to the soil.' (Of course she is – aren't all mothers?) Which explains why she's called me Lily, and my sister Poppy. It doesn't, however, explain why she's so barking MAD. Do other people's mothers hug trees when they go to the park?

No, because it is not normal.

When my brother came along she was stumped for a name. I suggested Cabbage or Potatohead. She accused me of being cruel and jealous. I told her I didn't know the meaning of the words.

Me? Cruel? Never! Why would I want a baby Potatohead? I don't even like potatoes. I like chips and crisps, but they aren't *really* potatoes.

Annoying as he is, I feel sorry for my little brother, Bay. Being called Bay must be worse than Cabbage. Sometimes Mum even forgets to call him Bay and shortens it to Tree, which is one letter longer if you can count. Besides, Tree is not a name, it's a thing that grows out of the ground. You'd think somebody who watches as many gardening shows as Mum might know that, but then there are many things on this planet that are clearly here to confuse and confound me.

Have you noticed how flowers, and even some things you put in salad, are girls names? Rose, Hyacinth (what a nightmare), Lily, Jasmine, Sorrel, Marigold, Lettice. At least I'm not called Poppy. Heroin is made from poppies. Clearly our parents are the ones who are cruel. I've told them not to be surprised when Poppy ends up a junkie.

I'm standing in the kitchen, minding my own business, when Mum comes out with, 'Please don't be so angry, little Lilylah.' I hate it when she calls me that. But still, better than my sister's pet names: Poppypoops and Popsicle.

Mum's current obsession is *my* anger. 'I know your father leaving to live with his secretary wasn't very nice, but we must find it in our hearts to forgive him.' She says this while viciously pulling apart a head of lettuce.

'OK,' I say, and whisper under my breath, '*Courage, mon*

ami!' Sometimes only French will do to express my feelings of intense frustration. (Plus, I need the practice as I intend to live in Paris when I am a megastar. *J'adore Paris*.)

Later on, Mum's in the garden chopping wood with all her might, shouting, 'Lying bastard'. Then she's back into the house, full of smiles, glugging down a few glasses of wine and smoking a couple of fags, before stating, 'Ah, now that's better. Why don't I make a nice friendly salad for supper?'

Can you imagine anyone describing salad as: 1) Nice or 2) Friendly? *Incroyable!* Mum's off the deep end big time.

'Why are you chopping wood, Mum? *Pourquoi?* We have no fireplace, and besides, it's summer.'

'I'm thinking of putting one in. A wood-burning stove.'

'But you're chopping the dining chairs, and there are only three left.'

'I've never liked those chairs. I want your father to buy us new ones. I've seen some in Conran, bargains at only two hundred pounds each. I mean, if your father can hire a yacht to drift around the Mediterranean . . . what's a few chairs?'

'Mediterranean . . . What? Dad said it was a work trip!'

'Ah well, Lily, your father doesn't always tell the truth. I suppose you'll have to learn that some time.'

Mum Loves FishMan

The summer holidays have started and I think it's time to escape. Beam me up, Scotty, please. There isn't room for me, not in this madhouse. There isn't even a chair for me. I tell Mum this and she says, 'Can't you ever think about anyone but yourself? It's just me, me, me, with you. Why do you always have to be so unutterably selfish?'

'*Moi?* Selfish? *Je ne comprend pas!*'

'Lily!' she growls like an incontinent Pekinese. 'English!'

'In English then. I'm not the one who asked the young hippy from the corner café out, in front of the whole neighbourhood. I'm not the one who dribbled with delight from the corner of my mouth when he said yes.'

Anyone who witnessed it would know it was past embarrassing – it was disgusting.

'What?' she says. 'He's just . . . my new friend.' She then smiles creepily.

What is it with old parents chasing younger 'friends'? I have to ask her. 'Why did you have to do that, Mum?' Sometimes it's important to understand why parents enjoy humiliating you.

'You only live once, and Adrien and I are still coursing with the lifeblood of passion. We recognise the creative surge in each other. You seem to forget, Lily, we're young and attractive. Why shouldn't we live and love?'

'But you're so not. I mean, OK, you're still quite pretty.

But Mum, haven't you noticed his scaly hands? He's not called FishMan for nothing.'

'He's not called FishMan, Lily! Actually he has a very nice . . .'

'Don't tell me. No. I don't want to know. *C'est dégueulasse.*'

'I was going to say touch. Yes, he has a very nice touch, not at all . . . reptilian.' She giggles frighteningly.

'That's what I was afraid you were going to say. You mean aquatic anyway, not reptilian.'

'Whatever. I like him. He makes me laugh and he's so . . . musical.'

'Mum, he makes us laugh too, but not in a good way. Don't see him any more, I beg you. *C'est trop ennuyeux!*'

'I'll tell you what's boring. The pretentious predictability of your French phrase book. Can't you find any new . . . phrases?'

'You don't appreciate my linguistic ability! You have no respect for France . . . Anyway, it's not normal. Nobody else's mother in the street goes out with FishMan Gill from the caff.'

'It's a wine bar.'

'It's a caff. You could do so much better. Can't you go out with someone with a real job? I'll help – I'll give you a makeover. We'll find a man on the Internet. You aren't bad looking, and if we did your hair, changed your clothes – *c'est bonne maman!*'

'*Bonne maman*? I'm not a pot of jam. You're being ridiculous again. Go to your room.'

'I'll call ChildLine, and report your strange cruelty!'

'To your room, before I explode, Miss Lily!'

'*Zut alors! Mademoiselle Lily, merci beaucoup!*'

'Why did I ever let you go to France? Why?'

My Heart's Secret Exposed!

Mum has gone completely crazoid, bonkers, barking, barmy. Well, nothing new there. She's said I should go and live with Dad as soon as he gets back tomorrow, that I'm getting 'impossible'.

Tant pis! Whatever! (What's 'whatever' in French?) I am perfecting a pleasing door slam. Might have to try that one more time.

'Lily!'

And again.

'Lily! You're making your brother cry.'

I am living in a perfectly nice, baby-blue painted, two-storey house with purple passion flowers growing up the outside, and we've even got a beautiful palm tree in the garden. In the summer we always have sunflowers and giant daisies growing in our front garden and it takes two minutes for me to get to Battersea Park in south London, with only the Thames dividing us from Chelsea. Which just proves how deceptive appearances are because I am actually living in a madhouse, with a nutter mother, a screaming Bay – and Poppy, another nightmare altogether. Don't let me get started on the Impossible Poppy.

Yesterday, she kidnapped my diary. When I asked for it back she wouldn't give it to me. I was reasonable and calm.

'Here, little junkie, give my diary back and I'll give you drugs.' I shook some cough drops at her. She didn't. I heard the door lock and through it I could hear her laughing and howling like the beast of Bodmin as she kept reading bits out through her window to passers-by below.

When she reappeared, she prodded me with her finger saying, 'I'm telling Billy you love him.' Knowing my luck, I thought, he had probably already heard. She then started to sing, if you can call it that. It was more of a howl: 'Billy and Lily sitting in a tree, K-I-S-S-I-N-G. First comes babies then comes marriage . . .'

'And-then-you-have-your-throat-torn-out,' I added playfully.

Boy Oh Boy

Billy is our next-door neighbour. He's sixteen, and the fittest thing for miles. He rides a bike and he has this blond hair that falls in a curl into his eyes, and his . . .

well, I could go on forever about Billy, his blue eyes and the way just one cheek dimples when he smiles . . . One day I'll have a boyfriend and he'll be Billy, or just like Billy . . . But if Poppy tells him, I'll die. Truly. I might as well kill myself now. Is there any point in waiting for my life to end? It's already over . . .

Naturally I had to do something. I got the axe from the garden shed to convince her to give back my diary, and she went screaming to Mum saying that I was trying to kill her. Honestly!

Overreacting is Poppy's forte. *Excusez-moi*, but did I *use* the axe? No. Did I kill her? No. Can I dream? Yes.

If she's not going to die, Poppy plainly deserves an excruciating life.

The Final Solution

I never thought I'd say it, but the summer holidays have already been way too long, cooped up with the loonygoon Lovitts. All my friends are away. Bea, my best friend, left a week before the end of term to stay with her grandparents in America, and I've got no one to talk to and too many people to shout at. Can't believe school only broke up the day before yesterday. Only fifty days to go.

I have to e-mail Bea, or follow Mum down the one-way street to Crazyville Central.

8

Subject: Life Over

Dear Bea,

Mum has checked into the Crazyville Motel – an inn with no way out. What is the big deal? I only left Bay in the playground in his buggy and came home without him. It wasn't my fault Billy started talking to me. How was I supposed to remember Bay when I was looking into Billy's eyes and he was looking into mine? Basically I am one smitten kitten. Anyway, Bay was still there when I went back to fetch him, blissfully dribbling at the trees, babbling rubbish to the squirrels, the usual. Maybe Bay is a tree, a nut tree and that's why the squirrels like him? I know where he gets the nuttiness from . . . The upshot is, Mum says she's chucking me out, that I have to live with Dad. Dad, obviously terrified, comes up with what he calls, 'the final solution'. He brings over some rank brochures that he's got off the net, for boot camp. Is this legal? Ask your Grandad, isn't he a lawyer?

Basically my life is over. Moannnnn. Are you having a nice time? Miss your royal buzziness. Arghhhh – or as they say climbing up the Eiffel Tower, *'Je suis très fatigué!'* Know wot I mean?

Love U,

Lily xxxx

In fact the conversation about boot camp was far worse than I could describe to Bea. Mum was utterly unreasonable.

'So kind of you to retrieve your brother, Lily. Why are you so irresponsible? Don't you realise Bay could have been abducted?' Mum was as irritable as a sunbathing mole.

'No. He couldn't – who'd want him?'

'It's pointless talking to you. And don't eat a chocolate sandwich just before dinner.'

'But I'm starving to death.'

'Wait for dinner.'

'I'll die. Do you want me to die, Mum?'

'Don't be so stupid. Lay the table.'

'Stupid! Mum, what's the matter with you? I need food, this is a crucial growing period and you're depriving me. Are you trying to give me eating disorders?'

'I have had enough of you, Lily. This is it. Enough.'

'What's wrong with you, Mum? Are you taking drugs?'

'I'm calling your Dad. Now! You are driving me insane.'

'Maybe you need therapy Mum? Might be a good idea.'

'Lil-l-yy!'

And shortly after that, Dad arrived with the brochures.

'Summer camp? You mean boot camp!' I screamed. 'You're sending me away because you all hate me.'

'We don't hate you . . . we just think you'll be happier . . . safer with other people your own age for the summer. It's a lovely summer holiday camp in the Lake District.'

'I don't want to be locked away in a tent in the wilderness, I'll be eaten by wild bears. Stop doing those looks.' Then it dawned on me. 'It's a mental home, isn't it?' My parents gave each other more looks, as if I couldn't see. 'Now calm down,' said Dad. Is there any sentence in the English language guaranteed to make you less calm? 'It's a mixed summer camp. Boys and girls. Lots of multi-activities to make you more motivated and involved.'

'You mean mixed up. Great.'

'It's about helping you to find your inner happiness, Lilylah.' Mum gulped down her wine and poured herself more. 'It's nice, that's why it's called CampHappy.'

'I don't have any inner, or outer, happiness. Mum, can't you see? I'm fried to misery, like a piece of your bacon.' I thought this might inspire sympathy in Dad because Mum's 'burning' (it would be so wrong to call it cooking) had always driven him mad. But nothing. I tried again. 'Can't you see? I'm stuck in a torpor of tragedy.'

Instead of pity or remorse, they both started laughing insanely.

'Can you adults not take *anything* seriously?'

'We'll write,' Mum said brightly. 'It's only for twenty-one days. At least you get a holiday.'

'Dad promised we'd go to France! We always go to France.'

'I can't fit it in this summer too much work on. Another time,' he said.

'Well, my life's over anyway. Like anything I say makes any difference. I could lie down in the road and wait for the number 77 bus to pulp me on its way to Clapham. Can we at least get a takeaway for my last meal?'

I was actually more concerned about Billy than food. How was I going to get to know him if I wasn't near by? This is the proof I need to submit to the Royal Society for Prevention of Cruelty to Children – I mean the NSPCC. But I wonder if the RSPCA would be interested, seeing as I'm being treated like a dog?

'That's settled then,' Dad carried on enthusiastically. 'It'll be a rest for us all.'

'It'll be lovely, all that camping and ponies. Lucky you!' Mum added.

'Yes, lucky you, Lily,' Poppy (evil betrayer), walking into the living room, sneered sarcastically.

'Just one question. How come Poppy's not going too?'

'Because I have a summer job as a waitress at the Chelsea Café, and I've got A-level course work to do. Besides, I'm not an evil, angry, axe-wielding witch like you.'

I got up to strangle her, but Dad pushed between us and said, 'Lily! Look at the pictures,' waving the brochures and trying to distract me.

'I can read you know.'

I immediately wished I couldn't. I knew my fate as soon as I read the introduction:

The Professor and his team at CampHappy want teenagers to gain resilience, self-esteem, self-reliance and social awareness as they move into adulthood. With a series of fun, structured activities . . .

HELP!

'You can't send me to boot camp. It's against the European Convention of Children's Human Rights,' I cried out, but Mum was shoving a Conran brochure in Dad's face as he played with Bay.

'What's wrong with Habitat chairs? They've got a sale on,' Dad moaned.

'*Your* furniture came from Conran. If it's good enough for you, it's good enough for us. And, by the way, the car needs servicing and Lily needs camp gear, and Poppy needs . . . a coat.'

'But it's July, Jenny. Can't the coat wait?'

'No. There's been some very nasty weather recently.'

'How much is it all going to cost?'

'Cheaper than a yachting holiday in Cannes without the kids.'

'Jenny, that's so unfair. You know it was work.'

'Was it?'

Ah . . . At times like this it's just like having Dad back home.

'Well I'd better be getting back.'

'Absolutely. Go. Go and leave a cheque. Don't keep *her*, waiting.'

I tried again, panicked that it seemed to have been decided. 'You can't send me away. I'm not a piece of furniture you can put into storage when you go off it. It's against the European Convention of Children's Human Rights. And Dad, why didn't *we* go on the yacht? Why aren't we going to Granny's in France? I could go by myself.' My final trump card I save till last. 'I miss Granny. I bet she misses me too.' I sniffed sadly.

'I'll pick you up and drive you down to the station on Saturday morning.' Dad staple-gunned a kiss on my forehead. 'Monster,' he added.

I made a hideous gargoyle face, all bitter and twisted, like the ones around the Notre Dame Cathedral in Paris. Nobody noticed. They didn't listen. Sometimes I wonder if I'm the invisible girl. My talent is utterly wasted on them.

As Dad drove away, Bay came up and gave me his potty. I know he was trying to be nice, but the last thing I needed to smell was some of his poo. 'I want to see Granny. Go away, Bay. I don't want your poo. You're disgusting.'

Potatohead threw the potty and mess over the carpet and started bawling. I'm never having kids.

Predictably, Mum said, 'Lily, clean up that mess. Look what you've done to poor Bay!'

Nothing compared to what *they'll* do to him in time, I thought, escaping upstairs.

My Future Is Hollywood

I am resigned to the fact that my family don't want me. Well, I will show them. One day I will become really famous, and *très riche*. I'll return, saying, *'Je suis un rock star'*, or *un mega film star* (but nothing that involves operations like breast enlargements as am *très* squeamish). Then they'll have to pay to talk to me.

Then, when I'm grown up, they'll all be begging to live with me in my superstar villa with pool, but by then I'll be surrounded by lackeys and I won't need them. I could give them the pool house, but I'll probably need it for the pool boy.

I won't be staying long in boot camp. After a week they'll see how boring life is without me and they'll want me back.

L'Amour Est Mort

Saturday morning arrives and still no mention of seeing Granny in Menton in southern France. Mum tries to tell me that Granny is away, as if that was a likely reason for breaking the annual family tradition – how am I going to keep up my immaculate French or pass my exam, or live in Paris? My parents aren't content with ruining the present, they're trying to sabotage my future too.

Mum hugs and kisses me, as if she doesn't want to let me go, and then when I'm in the car she gives me a copy of *Vogue*. She must have me confused with some millionaire's child who buys Chanel handbags. Poppy says she'll send me e-mails and gives me an old copy of *The Face* with my favorite singer, Lockett, smeared over the cover, looking more gorgeous than . . . gorgeous.

'*Pourquoi?*' I ask her, pretending I don't know why she'd give me such an exquisite thing. Billy is my possible passion, Lockett is my secret, impossible passion, *mon petit choufleur amour*. 'My little cauliflower love' doesn't sound quite the same, but French does lovely things even to vegetables, or as we say *en français, légumes*. Even *légumes* sounds so much sexier than any human body part in English.

'You want to marry him – I read it in your diar-rhoea, May 5th. Ha ha!'

'Isn't it time for your medication, Miss-Take-in-the-Community?' I snap back.

'Now girls,' Mum interrupts in a soothing voice. 'You'll upset your brother.'

I stare back, brave, yet desolate. (I love it that in France when somebody bumps into you, they say, '*Pardon, je suis désolée!*' The French are officially *crazee!* Why would you be desolate from bumping into someone?)

'*Pis allez!*' I shout at them to go away as Dad drives off, but they just keep smiling and waving like happy idiots. I am beginning to understand how Marie Antoinette felt on the guillotine, but worse is waiting for me as we drive around the corner.

My heart quickens when I catch sight of Billy – until I see he is busy making a sandwich, leaning that tart Amanda (Year Ten) against the café wall. How could he? When he could have me, he chooses her. She looks like a giant piece of ham with nasty cheese-string peroxide hair sticking out. Boot camp, death camp, what does it matter now? My life is over if I can't have Billy. *Tout l'amour est mort!* And I can't even e-mail Bea about this major tragedy!

The Meaning of Rubbish

Dad keeps trying to tell me about how exciting it's all going to be, while my heart is collapsing like a Rich Tea biscuit dunked in a hot cup of tea. This man has no sensitivity. Maybe he has no heart? He drones on about what happened at his boarding school – as if it's related or like I care? Like the time in a school ritual, they tied his feet to a loo chain, and flushed the loo on his head. He says this laughing!

'Remind me. Just how am I related to you?' I ask,

because if things are hereditary I am very afraid. As it is I look like my mum, which isn't too bad, but why do I have her tiny nose, monster mouth, curly hair, a bum the size of mount Everest and breasts that start at my neck and won't stop growing. Imagine being old and having to wear the biggest bra in the world ... And, if my bum keeps growing and my sense of humour is my father's ... I'm doomed. I hope someone invents lyposuction surgery for my dad's sense of humour (or will he have to get his brain drained?). Anyway, what's the point of it all, if boys like Billy prefer ham like Amanda?

My face is pressed to the window as we leave Battersea Park and its golden Buddha behind us and drive over Chelsea Bridge. I wonder about asking Dad to stop the car. I could solve everything by jumping off the bridge and into the river, but I'm put off by the nasty sludge-brown water, and interrupted by Dad.

'No need to be so sarcastic, Lily. By the way, Suzi bought you the bag in the back. I think it's make-up and rubbish. Why you'd want to ruin your face with muck, God knows.'

'Well, at least *someone* understands,' I say, reaching into the bag and picking out some gorgeous lip-gloss. 'Dad, did they have dictionaries when you were at school? This isn't rubbish, it's fantabuloso, *fantastique*!'

Disgusting Dads

Suzi is Dad's twenty-two-year-old live-in girlfriend. I know I should hate her because Dad left Mum when she was pregnant with Bay. Not nice. But the problem is, Suzi has great taste, the best clothes, and we're almost the same size. It feels mean to Mum for me to like her, but what can I do? Suzi is really fun, clever, sweet, pretty and an artist who lives in this groovy loft apartment in Brick Lane. So why's she with Dad? She told me once, 'I had to earn some money so I got a job as a secretary and I fell in love . . .' (yuck). Still, Suzi is great, she's always giving me gorge stuff. Poppy won't go near her, and Mum won't let Dad have Bay to stay, so what am I supposed to do – hate her or love her? I know – why don't I be friends with everyone? Good idea? I'd put Mum, Dad and Suzi in the same room, light the blue touch paper and stand well back. I've never liked fireworks or arguments. Why can't adults grow up and stop fighting?

In the Bag

There's red nail polish, black and white mascara, a mammoth Toblerone and a polka dot notebook, but best is a retro American T-shirt with *Trucker Girl* written across a huge red truck.

'Oh my God. I love it. Thank Suzi so much. *C'est incroyable.*' Already Billy is fading from my mind. Presents are a wonderful invention.

'Ah, *oui oui*, a little *anglais*, a little *français*. I'm, how you say, so glad you like them, my *cherie*,' Dad says in the worst French accent ever spoken.

Hard to believe his mum, my Granny, lives in Southern France and we've been going there every summer since I was born. Dad believes that if you just put on a weird accent, all foreign waiters throughout the world will understand you. *Quel dommage!*

'Father, I am so very happy we're not going away together to France after all; your accent is embarrassing.'

'Lily! I'd hardly be absconding with you alone. You're my daughter!'

'Eww, Dad! Does Suzi know you're like some rank incesty-pedo! Yuck!'

'Thank you, daughter, I love you too.'

Euston railway station appears and we turn off the main road away from the sun and into its grey gloom.

My stomach is jitterbugging as we head onto the platform for the train to Lancaster. I'm scared. What if I'm going to the House of Dracula and not CampHappy? Dad doesn't help.

He hugs me as the train pulls up. 'You're my darling daughter, my favourite Lily in the world. Remember that.'

'Where do you send the Lilys you don't like?' I want to say, but you always think of the best things too late. All I manage is a last minute plea. 'Why can't we go to France this summer, Dad?'

'Lily, don't start. I've told you, I've got too much work on. Ring Mum when you arrive.'

'What if they don't let us and they send us to Belgium to be Internet porn stars, and keep us locked in a dungeon. What will you do then?'

'You're hardly joining the white slave trade. It's a few weeks in the Lake District. I put some credit on your phone and here's some extra money.' Nothing makes me feel better, not even the feel of fresh bank notes. 'Hey, that girl looks about your age, let's go and talk to her.'

My father accosts the stranger, who, *quelle surprise*, doesn't know about CampHappy, because she is part of a normal family going on holiday together.

On the train they stare at me with a mix of sympathy and fear. I demolish the Toblerone and spend the rest of the journey, fist in mouth, picking out bits of nougat from my back teeth and trying not to think about what might lie ahead for me. Of course I could run away, hitchhike to Paris, but I think I'd better work on my French first.

CampHappy. How hard can it be?

CHAPTER TWO

J'arrive – Looking Cool, Feeling a Fool

I am fully immersed in my usual Day-Dreaming Mode (DDM). I am a musical star with the voice of Billie Holiday (why does everything remind me of Billy?), resting in my trailer, make-up and wardrobe fussing over me. Billie Holiday was this incredible jazz singer of the 1940s who makes every song either drip with joy, or die of sadness. So, in my head, I'm singing to my entourage 'Ain't Nobody's Business if I Do', (my current theme tune), when I glance out of the window as the train slows. The train stops and I am caught between my dream and real life (which is a female crazoid, madly grinning, waving a CampHappy placard). And then it strikes me: I am not yet a film star! With no flunkeys to do it for me, I have to fling open the door, and pull my cases after me. Of course it is a cold, grey, dreary, drizzle of a day. Why does it always rain on miserable days? *Alors!*

Reality stinks compared to my daydreams, and this weather makes my normally long, straight hair curl up and frizz. Who says real life is better than fiction? Mum says if I stopped daydreaming, I could partake in real life. Great. That'll be another scream to look forward to. Still, I promised her that I would make an effort (against my better judgement and usual behaviour) and be thoroughly involved at CampHappy . . .

Why did I promise such a thing? The last time I looked at real life, Billy and Amanda morphed into a giant cheese and ham sandwich.

'Call me Ann,' Crazoid says in hyper breathlessness, interrupting my thoughts. 'I'm Head Coordinator. Now, I must rally the troops – wait here.'

'Coordinator of what? Bad glasses, breath and hair?' I wittily reply under my breath. She scurries off down the platform like an anoraked hamster. I must remember to write some of these hilarious sayings down in my new notebook. That was what Oscar Wilde did, then twiddled them into plays and made a fortune – before being sent to prison for being a homosexual and dying, impoverished, in a Parisian garret.

Obviously, I'm not going to copy *all* his lifestyle choices, because I've got to be a megastar. But I will go out with beautiful boys and live in Paris, so we are similar in some ways. Weirdly, the garret he died in is the very height of posh chic now. Mum pointed it out when we went on the Eurostar last Easter and said, before I even asked, that there wouldn't ever be a chance that we could stay there, now Dad has spent all the family money on Suzi.

I wouldn't mind ending up at L'Hotel, like old Oscar. As he said so sweetly – and is written on his statue in Adelaide Street, next to Trafalgar Square, London, Centre of the Universe – 'We are all lying down in the gutter, but some of us are looking up at the stars.' On my good days, I intend to *be* one of those stars; on the bad days, I think I'll be lying in the gutter too, looking up at the stars.

As I wait on the platform I dream of L'Hotel, of hiring Poppy as my personal assistant, and of hot and cold running champagne. I wonder what hot champagne's like to bathe in? Sticky? Would the bubbles all pop?

When Ann reappears she's with two of the buffest boys, like *ever*. One is blond and tall with great floppy hair, while the other is dark and incredibly fit, shorter with curly hair and chocolate button brown eyes. I hope they weren't sitting on the same train as me. Shock *horreur*! I'd die if they saw me picking Toblerone out of my teeth. What if bits are still there? Must not show teeth at all costs. Where is Bea when I need her? Skiving off to America. What's the point in having best friends when they aren't available for commiseration at life's crucial breaking points? Bea is officially sacked for being vacant from duty. Not really. Bea's the best. She's bringing me back gallons of beautilicious chocolate syrup (no chocolate in it, but better than chocolate and maybe even boys).

These aren't just boys though, they are gorgeous and standing next to me. Sometimes the mysteries of the universe pull together to confound and delight me, *je pense* . . .

At least I changed into my Trucker Girl T-shirt on the train, and I have on my new red Converse boots and extra-tight jeans (which cunningly reduce my bum from Everest to molehill in three buttons – sly, huh! Worth every penny that Suzi spent on them. Dadgirlfriendthingies are a valuable asset).

I push my aviator sunglasses up to rest in my hair, so I can see their eyes better (and so they can see mine). If you look straight into someone's eyes and they look back, I'm sure it's a sign of possible interest. There is also a better chance that they won't be looking at the Toblerone in your teeth. Of course the glasses fall off the back of my head into a puddle. *Je ne suis pas amusée. Très* uncool. I can see them sniggering. If the train wasn't standing in the way, I would throw myself onto the rails.

'This is William, and this is Blake. William Blake. Very

good. William Blake – the poet? Never mind,' Ann says. 'This is Daisy.'

I had begun to feel sorry for her in those clothes, but calling me Daisy put an end to that. Do I *look* like a Daisy?

'I'm Lily actually.' I can't look directly at the boys, and so look to one side and realise there is a girl standing quietly with them. She is small, not much bigger than Polly Pocket, dressed all in black with dark straight hair, a moon-pale face and the unblinking eyes of an owl. She reminds me of someone . . . someone spooky.

'Hi, Lily,' Spooky Girl says.

'Yeah, hi,' say the boys, waving their hands like paddles back.

Ann laughs it off. 'Sorry, Lily. Oh you know, they're both flowers. Don't be surprised if next time I call you Rose or Tulip.' She laughs again. Just who is meant to be the adult here? 'Last but not least is Maya,' Crazoid says, turning to Spooky Girl. 'Such original names. Were you named after the Indians?'

'No, my mother. She died giving birth to me,' Maya retorts, completely straight-faced, to Ann – but she turns to us, winks and smiles. I like this girl.

'Oh dear,' says Ann. 'You must excuse . . . well, let's all get out to the Land Rover and get to CampHappy. I can feel we're all going to get on. Maya, I thought I spoke to your mother? I must have been wrong. Never mind. My intuition says we'll be great friends. I always listen to my intuition, it never lets me down. Now have we got everything? Keys? Did I put my bag down? No, sorry, on my shoulder, silly me. Off we go. Yes, lots of fun . . .'

The woman is bonkers. She looks like a scarecrow but her brains are in a far worse mess. To think our parents have entrusted our safety to this woman.

We spend the journey listening to her wittering on as we drive up and down through the lush, green, damp countryside. I know it's supposed to look nice, but there is something spooky about the lack of buildings and humans in the countryside. All the way there we are trying not to laugh at Ann, until we get so lost that we have to do the map reading. How had she got the 'Head Coordinator' job? I'm not letting her anywhere near my head. I'm happy when we finally get to the cute toytown village that looks like Noddy and Big Ears' home, and where the signs say that CampHappy is only half a mile away.

Reaching Base

Base Camp, as Ann calls it, was once a gorgeous country house before they gutted it and turned it into a youth offenders prison or loony bin, aka CampHappy. It still has a beautiful marble staircase that winds down into the main hall, with an excellent looking handrail for sliding down. It looks like butterscotch swirl being whipped through ice cream.

Ann leads us upstairs, to the dormitories that probably once had four-poster beds, but now have a unique 'designer' prison look of metal beds and grey blankets. The bathrooms are weird too. Who has six basins in a bathroom with three loos? Maybe you're supposed to wash one hand in each sink?

The boys are led off to the other side of the corridor, the west wing, by Ann, who insists that we can meet up soon in the communal sitting room, and later in the canteen, where high tea is served at six.

'When do we eat dinner?' I ask. I am starving. Dad hadn't even remembered sandwiches, and one large Toblerone is not enough to keep a growing girl growing, unless all I'm growing is spots.

'That is your evening meal. We call it high tea. Dinner you have at lunch time.'

'You do? So what do you call breakfast?'

'Breakfast.' She isn't amused, but Maya is. She crosses her eyes at me in sympathy. 'Well, I'll leave you two to unpack. The other girls are out potholing. When you've finished, come downstairs and there'll be a cup of tea, and buns if you're lucky.' She walks away, muttering to herself.

'Is that woman completely crazoid?' I say, turning to Maya. '"Don't be surprised if I call you Tulip or Rose!" I hope she's not surprised when I call her Table or Chair,' I mimic, bouncing on one of the four beds.

'I thought my Grandma was a loony but Ann beats her hands down. Which bed do you want?' Maya asks, gesturing at the cardboard-looking beds, and taking in the bare walls and cheap white manky furniture.

'I don't mind, though I prefer ones without people. Those two look taken.' Two beds in the middle of the room are strewn with clothes and magazines.

'Do you mind if I have the one by the window?'

'Sure. Do you think I can use this cupboard?'

'What, to sleep in?' Maya asks, as if I was planning something insane as I unpack.

'How long are you staying here?'

'Dunno. The usual, three weeks.'

'I've told my Dad he's got to pick me up if I don't like it,' Maya says.

'Why?'

'I don't like being away from home. I don't like staying away, I just don't. Not even hotels, all right?' She says this so maniacally that it makes me feel normal. I guess she feels just as insecure as I do.

Just because I hated things at home, didn't mean I wanted to leave home. But I have to cheer Maya up, so I say, 'It's OK, Maya. Really. Can't you see it's good to escape from our parents? I mean, I know it's weird being locked up with freaks, but it can't be any worse than that movie *One Flew Over the Cuckoo's Nest* about a loony bin. It might be funny. Actually, Ann has a lot in common with the psychotic nurse in the film . . . The more I think about it, the more I reckon that if you leave, we're all going to come with you. Your mum and dad wouldn't mind, would they?'

That got Maya laughing. 'Don't be ridiculous. We've only got a two-bedroom house in Chelsea.'

'I don't mind, I'm no snob. It'll be cosy.' I jump next to her on the bed. 'Twenty of us snugged up in one bed. The boys would have to sleep on the floor, but that can't be helped.'

'Get offa me, you crazy girl,' she says, laughing.

I kangaroo jump, bed to bed. 'Hey, only my psychiatrist can call me by my first name.'

'Do you really have your own psychiatrist?' Maya looks shocked.

'Of course not, my dad's too mean. One day, when I'm a star, I'll employ a full-time therapist to listen to my mother, sister, brother and dad. Then I won't have to. It's hard being the only sane one in the family, but there's got to be one normaloid.'

'Lily, you are weird.'

'Takes one to know one. I wonder what William and Blake are up to?'

'Dismembering each other, I expect, being boys!' I can tell she has less interest in the boys than me. I am not a sex-maniac-nympho-fiend, because I can go hours, sometimes days or weeks, without seeing Billy – I mean, a boy – I fancy, but then he appears, and I'm a smitten kitten. *L'amour, l'amour, l'amour!*

For a moment I had forgotten that I hate Billy. I really hate him. He is the ugliest, meanest thing in the whole of England. Make that the universe.

I have to cheer myself up, so I get some toothpaste to stick Poppy's magazine cover of Lockett over my bed, so I can say goodnight and good morning to something handsome. There's got to be some joy, and staying in CampHappy is so far neither Happy nor Camp. Oh, to be in Gay Paree, now *that's* camp.

It is my destiny to live in Paris. To wake each morning to *croissant, pain au chocolat* and *café au lait* in a back-street *petit café* with tobacco-stained walls and a chrome bar, like in my fave movie, *Amélie*. What can I say, *j'aime les berets*.

I finish unpacking in DDM (Day-Dreaming Mode), while Maya plays dead, leaving her bag untouched. My stomach growling brings me back to reality.

'Maya? Let's go and investigate the buns before the rest return.'

'I don't want to do anything. I want to go home.' Maya has it bad.

'I'm hungry and it'll be fun. Has anyone ever told you that you look like that actress?' I take her arm, dragging her up and out the door.

'In *The Addams Family*? Yes, constantly. At school they call me Wednesday, no matter what the day of the week.'

'No, I meant *The Bride of Frankenstein*. Actually, maybe you're more like *Bride of Chucky*. Ha ha, see you can laugh. It's allowed. Your mum isn't dead, is she?'

'Not from giving birth to me. I didn't have to kill her, she's brain-dead. Alcohol poisoning.' We walk out of the dorm and through the thread of the dark wood-panelled corridors. Maya's humour might be sicker than mine.

I try to lighten the mood a little.'Yeah, what is it with mums?' I say. 'My mum's always getting drunk and smoking cigarettes.'

'Why do they drink so much wine? Wine's disgusting. God, if I was allowed to do the shopping, I'd fill up on chocolate milk.'

'Or apple and mango juice. Yum.'

'Ginger beer too,' she says.

'Homemade lemonade,' I add. I have a passion for lemons, which Maya shares, I realise, when she says, 'Mmm, don't you love lemon tart?'

'*J'adore Tarte au citron, c'est delicieux*. That's what they call it in France, you know, *Tarte au citron*.'

'They call it that in Sainsbury's as well.'

We both burst out laughing and, as we get to the stairs, Maya suggests sliding down the banisters. There is an evil glint of mischief in her eyes, and I know we are going to be good friends.

'Do you suppose it's allowed?'

'Do you suppose I care?' And down she slides, side-saddle, like a seasoned professional, jumping nimbly off at the end.

Less sure of my balance, I straddle the thing and slide backwards down the banister and get a painful shock as my bottom collides with the rail end. It feels like I am being speared by a kebab stick. 'Ouch!'

'What on earth do you think you're doing?' a voice booms across the hallway. 'You've interrupted my discussion session! This is not a zoo for monkeys, or a circus for acrobats, do you understand? Would you do this in your own home? No . . .'

I am being shouted at by the condescending voice of the kindly, smiling Prof featured in the brochure.

He doesn't give me a chance to say anything, except 'Sorry'. I try to look contrite, while Maya hides by the side of the grandfather clock, giggling. I want to say, 'If we had such excellent banisters at home, I'd be rather better at it. I'd have had some practice.'

'Go to the Common Room,' he orders and then leaves.

Do they have a Posh Room, I wonder? For those who do not slide down banisters?

Buff Boys & Dead Girls

'That was so funny.'

'It was *so* not,' I say, pushing Maya through the Common Room door and straight into William, who is at the pool table trying for a shot.

'Hi, sorry about Maya,' I say to him. 'Her limb control is way out.'

'Thank you, Lily.' Maya looks cross.

William shrugs shyly. He is damned cute and his hair has a way of glinting like gold when the sun strikes it. He is holding a cue and his smile's all lopsided. I can feel myself slipping into DDM, separating me from the room. I have to speak before I drown in his lagoon-blue eyes.

'We've come in search of the phantom buns.'

'Well, you're not getting mine,' Blake says, laughing, at the other end of the pool table. 'I need mine for sitting on.'

Hilarious.

'I meant the cakes or whatever Ann was going on about. I'm starving. I haven't had lunch,' I add, to justify my greed.

'Here's some biscuits before you die of malnutrition.' Blake sniggers and throws a pack at me. 'What kind of funeral do you want?'

'I only said I was hungry, and you're trying to bury me.

Are you one of those pyromaniacs?' I ask him.

'A pyromaniac is someone who loves fire, you mean someone who loves dead people,' says Blake. 'There's a word for that – a necro, I think?'

I look at Maya, and in her deadpan voice Maya says. 'What kind of place is this? Lily's clearly a lunatic and you want to work in a mortuary? How long have you been practising necrophilia?'

'I meant someone who likes fire,' I interrupt. 'I want to be incinerated, not eaten alive by worms. Don't you?' I ask them all. William looks away and says nothing.

'Or fish. You're eaten by fish if you're buried at sea,' I add.

'Your body goes to the bottom of the ocean, and that's when the bottom feeders like crabs and lobsters eat you up. Might as well just eat the person and cut out the crabs,' Maya adds.

'Let me get this straight. You're saying that when I eat a crab sandwich I might be eating a human?' Blake stares in disbelief at Maya.

'Basically.'

Maya is funny. She has a way of looking at people from the corners of her eyes. She is self-contained, shy, but still assertive. Solid, when she's not so neurotic about being homesick. A living set of contradictions.

'That's A1 Crapology,' says Blake.

'All necros think that. I think you have a very promising career ahead of you, in a funeral parlour,' says Maya.

'Well you should know. Don't your family own one? Aren't you related to The Addams Family?'

'Don't worry, Blake. I know which dormitory you're in, for when Uncle Fester comes to collect your body later tonight.' She grins sweetly at him. He does a blood-curdling scream. When she turns to me, and I see her teeth, I understand why – she's been eating liquorice.

Blake shakes his head in disbelief. 'You are one scary witch.'

'Enough is enough,' I say. 'If we start quarrelling on the first day, imagine what it will be like in a week, let alone three?' I look at William, hoping he'll back me up, but he still doesn't say anything – just casts occasional shy glances at me. He's obviously the tall, blond, silent type. I hope his silence doesn't mean he's too stupid to talk, or too self-obsessed. Blake was obviously the short, dark, egotistical, mouthy one. I hope there aren't two egos to deal with.

'Hey, come on guys, as my mum says, "This is the first day of the rest of our lives and we've got to make being together a happy experience." What about a singalong-a-Lily – *I'd like to teach the world to sing . . .*'

They all turn on me to pelt me with stale biscuits – more deadly than bullets. Where was the Prof when I needed him?

The shower of ammunition stops with a knock at the door. 'Is the Prof psychic?' I thought. But no, it's Ann poking her head in. 'Ah! You are all getting on. Splendid. Any questions?' she says, while trying to disappear again.

'Any buns? You said there might be buns,' I ask, picking biscuit out of my hair.

'I said, if you were lucky there might be buns. Unfortunately, Cook forgot to get them in the supermarket today. Never mind – high tea's in half an hour. It won't kill you to work up an appetite.'

'Please, no more death,' I groan. 'I suppose we can always eat our hands.' I start biting my nails in desperation.

'Yes, good idea, wash your hands and you'll be ready to eat.'

And then she disappears.

Blake mimes a finger screwing into the side of his head. We all nod; she is officially doolally. William smirks silently. I am starting to wonder, perhaps he can talk but is hiding a Donald-Duck voice – or worse – Minnie Mouse. Or maybe he's had an accident with a helium balloon and hasn't spoken since. Oh, poor boy. There must be a cure for a boy so cute.

I want to take my mind off my gnawing hunger and William's medical problems, so I look for Maya. She's at the back of the Common Room, merging into one of the computers on a desk.

'What are you doing?'

'I'm e-mailing Dad to tell him I'm locked up in Bedlam with the raving loony party, and he's got to get me out.'

'OK. But remember if you go, I'll have no one to tease, or tell my greatest ghost stories to.'

'I'm joking, Lily. I am thirteen. I can stick it out a couple of days . . .' I know she's just trying to be brave.

'After all, if your parents died and you were orphaned – though obviously that's never going to happen,' I add quickly. I don't want to put a hex on them.

She blinks and calmly replies. 'I wouldn't mind that, as long as I got to keep the house. I like my things. You know, familiar things. I've lived there since I was born. But you can always get new parents. Of course, I'd want to keep my Nanny Meg.'

At last, I have met someone even less sentimental than me.

'You're funny,' I tell her. Though sometimes I'm not sure she's joking.

'Not really.'

'I suppose I ought to let mine know I arrived safely. They worry so. Parents just need continual emotional support. If I'd known what high maintenance they were going to be . . .'

'I know. I never would have had mine either.'

'Do yours do that projecting fear thing? You know, when they worry about you killing your sister, but it's them that need help?' I feel like I've known Maya forever. Maybe she was a proper, nice sister to me in a past life or something?

Maya blinks at me again. 'No, I'm an only child. You're *sure* you're not seeing a psychiatrist?'

'You know, I'm *not* sure. Maybe I am. Maybe I *am* the psychiatrist or maybe I'm completely, utterly, mind-bogglingly maddddddd? What do you think?'

'Certifiable,' she says with her most bored voice. 'I'm calling 999 now.'

Maya is great.

E-mail Duty

Hurrah! An e-mail from Bea. Good old Bea. If Maya was my sister in a previous life, Bea has been my best friend through many lives.

Subject: Bored boring boredom

LilyLaLa, trust me, camp would be a relief from the small town drear. Every day's the same . . . think about this – there are people, such as my grandparents, living this dullness their whole lives. Hey – what's 3 weeks? And as for your mum! Wanna swap? You'd have to clean your room! Have you forgotten Mum and her room

inspection every Tuesday night. I mean, why Tuesday? It's
so totally random. Gramps says sorry it's legal, parents
can send you to camp. Got to go, Grandma needs to
show me off at their cocktail party. It's just one long
party after another, in a really bad way . . . Have fun,
write soon.
Loving the Lily,
Buzzer Bea xx00xx
P.S. Wot's the talent up 2?

And there is one from Poppy.

Subject: Prison
Dear Sis,
Hope the penal system is to your liking. Don't worry, you
forgot to lock your room but I'll make sure Tree doesn't
wreck it. Mum had FishMan from the wine bar round for
dinner. They were holding hands! Which way to the
Vomitorium?
Thanks for leaving me your lip-gloss.
Princess Poppy xxx

I have no choice but to reply to Poppy immediately.

Re: hab
Dear Popsicle,
This isn't like your drug rehab centres. Dad didn't want you
jealous, but I'm staying with royalty, eating lobsters and
bathing in champagne. It would all be wasted on you . . .

But I'm enjoying it. Have to go for my massage, ice cream and sauna now.

Lots of love,

Lily xxx

P.S. Touch my lip-gloss and you'll die – I've poisoned it.

P.P.S. Did you know about Amanda and Billy?

I am about to reply to Bea when the gong goes, and Ann's strangulated voice sings out: 'High tea, high tea.' Besides, I can't write to Bea about William and Blake with them in the room.

Canteen

What can I say about the food that would do it justice? Would disgusting cover it? The sausages remind me of something in Bay's potty . . . swimming in grease, with grated carrot salad. *C'est dégueulasse!*

I have decided to invent the Orange and Carrot Diet. I will lose weight and look tanned and lovely (carotene overdose gives you an orange kind of tan – true). Even with this endless rain the whole camp thing won't be a total disaster. I'll probably be spotted in town and signed up by a top model agency, because my bottom will have evaporated to the size of a ladybird. I shall make my diet regime a fitness DVD and book, become a multi-millionaire health superstar in moments and

41

then move to Paris. That's my future settled.

I tell Maya, who whines, 'But I want to put on weight, not lose it.'

I hate people with that 'problem'. She swaps her orange and salad for my sausages and potatoes. If you really are what you eat, I'm seriously worried I might turn into a vegetable. Because there's no way I'm going near anything else this kitchen has to offer.

The gang of potholers hasn't arrived back yet, so instead of meeting them we're given a little lecture by Ann on a typical day in CampHappy, which seems to go somewhere along the lines of: activity, break, activity, break and so on. Activity seems to be said potholing or walking around watery, underground caves, swimming, canoeing, rock climbing, riding. Breaks are times when we eat or do whatever we want, provided we stay within the base camp grounds. She says there are fifty of us here and that we must make an effort to all get along. Where are the others? I wonder. Surely they can't all be stuck down some hole? Thank goodness for Maya, William and Blake – the rest of the new arrivals are very dodgy-looking. Far too sporty for my liking. They're wearing tracksuits.

Ann then makes us watch a James Bond film in the Common Room, to get us 'in the mood' for tomorrow's adventure. The four of us stick together. The film is *Goldfinger*, on for the millionth time.

'I refuse to do anything involving stripping naked and being painted gold,' I say. 'That's abuse! Pussy Galore dies like that in the film.'

Ann looks at me as if I'm the one who's doolally. Some deranged idiots start laughing. I'm almost certain Blake is one of them.

'Lily, it's only a film,' Ann chides. 'And I don't want to spoil it, but Pussy Galore doesn't die.'

'Yes, it's only a film, Lily,' they mimic and laugh, and I know they are not laughing at Ann. I'm not stupid. I know *someone* dies painted gold.

If I could be head of this asylum . . . Oh, the rules I'd impose.

CHAPTER THREE

Shopping Is Not a Replacement for Real Life – Discuss.

A gong bangs. A siren rings in my ear, followed by a shouting foghorn. Oh joy, it's Ann.

'Wakey wakey, rise and shine, hang your knickers on the line. It's seven o'clock, girls. Porridge for breakfast. Dress suitably – you've got a day of team activity.'

There are not many things that make me want to get up in the morning, but porridge and Ann's voice I know AREN'T two of them.

'I need more sleep, my brain hasn't stopped growing – it's a medical fact.' It took me forever to go to sleep in this strange room last night. I make like a pillow, but Ann pulls my cover off.

'Come on, girls.' She's got streaks of cruelty running through her, as subtle as lightning.

I pull the mop off my face. When it behaves I can call it

hair. 'OK, OK, bully, I'm up. Help me, someone!'

Ann leaves and two strangers come over and have the cheek to say, 'Who are you?'

'I'm Lily, that's Maya. Were you the ones they said were lost in the pothole?'

'Yup, they got us lost. Again. I'm Isabelle, by the way, but everyone calls me Belle. Oh, and this is my cousin Izzy – she's called Isabelle as well. It's confusing.'

'Hurry up, otherwise the boys eat everything and there's nothing left but cold porridge lumps,' says Izzy.

Maya moves at double the speed of sound and is out the door before I can find my knickers, let alone my hairbrush.

'Hey guys. Wait for me,' I say. But they are gone.

Whoever invented mornings should be shot. Official.

What does suitable dress mean? I wish I was home, curled up in bed, but who am I kidding? Bay usually wakes me by six-thirty a.m. to show me his potty contents.

I put my jeans and flip-flops on and a T-shirt that says, 'Just Say NO!' Good advice for anyone here. Suitable for every occasion. The hairbrush is playing hide and seek, so I take my hair, wind it into a bun and stick a pencil through to hold it in place, therefore looking *très chic et très artistic. Voila!* Matisse himself would have approved.

Not that anybody notices downstairs. There are loads

more people in the canteen than the night before. I can't see what their faces look like, apart from the obvious similarities to pigs at a trough.

Izzy was right about the food. What is left is bacon fat swimming in – hmm, is that bacon fat or dandruff scum? No need to bother with lip-gloss today. The sausage is directly related to last night's dinner, some cold, hard cardboard is trying to impersonate toast – but I think in a crisis it could double as paving slabs – and the porridge looks like liquid concrete. I don't mind porridge made my way but this is something else. All porridge should be made with milk. Add golden syrup until it starts to separate. Eat until stomach splits from pleasure, not pain.

'Is there any orange juice?'

'No. Here's an orange, squeeze your own,' Cook says, giving me a banana. He laughs. Comedian.

I take a piece of cardboard, plastering it with marmalade – if it could do for Paddington Bear, I could survive on it. I get a cup of tea and sit down with Maya, Belle and Izzy.

'I told you so,' Izzy says, smirking as I chew the slab of 'toast'. Why do people always have to prove they are right? It's so annoying.

It looks like I was right about the food here. My dreams of dieting are coming true – but I should be careful what I wish for. I write a Post-it Note in my head for later.

Dear God,
I know you do lots of nice things, but can't you take a joke?
I'm starving. I really don't want to do a diet DVD – ever.
Lots of love,
Lily xxx

Conference

Our post-breakfast meeting is held in the Common Room. This is the first time we see who is in our team. Apart from Maya, William, Blake and me, there is also Izzy and Belle. The others are Rosie and Fiona, who are best friends and whisper in a corner together constantly like Siamese twins, Ian, who's quite chatty, Tony, very quiet, and Ben and Sam, who are nerdy male versions of Rosie and Fiona.

Apparently, we have to do this every day. 'Get together for a Confab', says Gordon, the rock-climbing guy. I know that's what he does because he wears a badge that says, *I ♥ climbing rocks.* He has a beard. He reminds me of the FishMan and that makes me feel a little sick.

I ♥ climbing Gordon says, 'Call me ClimbMeister'. He sits us all down and says, because some of us are new, we will have to have an induction day. 'Let's see how well you can swim, shoot, fly, die, that sort of thing. Only kidding, you're all safe with us.'

Funny guy! Has he not heard humans have a natural fear of dying?

The other leader for our team of twelve is Jackie, who can't stop jumping – I am wondering if she is ill, or has a pogo stick inserted up her bum.

Jackie is Australian and, obviously, the JumpMeister – 'Hey guys, let's jump to it, run down to the lake and splash around. Yeah! Who's for getting out canoes? Let's hear it for the canoes! Jump if you love canoes!'

It's exhausting just looking at her. Realistically, how is it possible, or normal, to get that excited over a canoe? What if Ann, the Prof, ClimbMeister Gordon and JumpMeister Jackie were normal when they first arrived? I start to worry that this freaky place has an evil spirit that turns everybody backward. Help! In three weeks I might regress to being Bay's age but stuck with my enormous bosoms, backside and hair, and tiny shrivelled brain the size of walnut. Is that scarier than joining the white slave trade as my dad suggested? I'm not so sure.

'Lily, have you been listening to anything I've said?' Jackie asks, blinking at me like she has an eye infection.

'Yes.' How can I tell her I switch automatically to DDM if not suitably entertained?

'What have I said?'

'That we should . . . We should all try to love . . . jumping? More?'

Everyone laughs, including Maya.

'Calling Lily to planet Earth? Go get the canoeing

48

stuff with the others, and change into your swimsuit.'

'*D'accord, très bien!*'

'Lily, why are you speaking French?'

Subject: Brain Damage

Dear BuzzBea,

Camp life is not all you cracked it up to be yesterday. I spent three hours of my life getting soaked in a canoe with very ugly yellow un-waterproofs and a hideous helmet on, making my hair a disaster. What am I supposed to be learning from this? I could have stayed in the shower for the morning as a banana, instead of being dressed as a lemon.

To be fair, though, it was quite fun, especially when I won a race at the end. Hurrah! All Hail the Royal Lily – for she is Queen of All the Woodland (and Water, Sea, Mountains, etc.). Then there was archery (I am almost Robin Hood!) and an induction to climbing – why oh why?

The boys seem not to like being beaten. Strangely I don't think they have realised that WE are the superior gender and we, like Boadicea, are here to teach them a thing or two.

Teaching boys like William is quite nice. He is really gorgeous and blond, a bit of a prince, but never says anything. Either he is dumb or has a voice like Goofy on Helium. And then there's Blake, who is also *très magnifique*, but he is so rude. He thinks it is funny to laugh at me when my T-shirt is soaked and my bosoms have nowhere to hide. I suspect all the boys (there are four others in our group –

Ian, Tony, Ben and Sam) hate me, as I am the world's fastest canoeist.

Sadly, I might be dead before you get this as the food is so fantasmagorically revolting as to be totally inedible. I am on lunch break. Lunch didn't take long as I am surviving on oranges because they can't ruin them. All the girls in my room (Izzy, Belle and Maya) give me theirs so I might live, but I'm warning you, I will soon have sunset orange skin and be as tiny as a small flower – a baby lily?

At least you get Tootsie rolls and Hershey bars, and you can spend all day in the mall shopping . . . Here I don't think they know what a shop is. We went through the village. They certainly don't understand the concept of food. I'm starting to dream of Mum's cooking, oh the burnt offerings of home comfort . . .

Lots of love,

(the wilting) Lily xxx

P.S. Is it possible to teletransport some Twinkies via e-mail? Pretty please, I will be your best friend until global warming gets us all.

P.P.S. Billy has taken up with Amanda, Year Ten! Imagine!

Bea must still be alive because a few minutes later, as I am checking my other e-mails, I get this:

Subject: Shopping is not a replacement for real life – Discuss.

Dear Plant head,

Shopping is not a replacement for real life. You would

know that if you were stuck here in a retirement village.
Much as I love Grandma and Gramps, none of their friends
are under 108. Now try imagining what the fashion is like
in the local mall. We have all the latest in designer zimmer
frames and giant nappies.

As much as I love you, I can't send Twinkies. I have tried to
squash the Twinkie into the computer but Gramps is saying I
must put it into my mouth. At least you'll have the pleasure
of knowing that I have enjoyed it for you, and don't say I
never tried. You will be skinny-girlinky, with long legs and big-
banana-feet when we go back to school, and I will look like
someone has inflated me with an electric pump. That is the
last Twinkie I am ever eating, until the next one. Oh hell,
nothing to do. I might as well go shopping and see some
movies in the mall, and eat a couple of buckets of popcorn.
They don't seem bothered about age restrictions, which is
nice. Of course I could just put me lil' ol' feet up and watch
reruns of *I Love Lucy*, and eat buckets of ice cream. Why does
all food come in buckets here? Because they haven't
discovered plates. Boom boom! Shopping might not be a
replacement for real life, but who needs real life, right?
Love,
The Bea xxx
P.S. Hey, snog some boys for me – you won't know which
one I would like, so snog them all . . . any of them would
be better than low-life Billy.

I reply quickly.

Subject: Sickie

Dear Mammoth Bea,

Are you sure they've built a plane small enough to fly your Twinkie bum back? You know you can eat as many buckets as you like and your tum remains as flat as Holland, very flat indeed.

Lots of love,

(The elegant) Lily xxx

P.S. They are trying to make us go out shopping for groceries. This is clearly slave labour. But the boys are quite nice.

After this fun, I have just enough time before afternoon activity to write quickly to Mum and Suzi. Am I evil thinking of them in the same thought?

Subject: Camp

Dear Suzi,

Thank you so much for pressies.

Tell Dad I am exhausted and miserable. They have made me do more than any person is meant to do. Plus there is no food and I am now so thin none of my clothes fit me – except the Trucker Girl T-shirt, which of course I love. The mascara too. Tell Dad the Prof is complaining because I am walking about practically starkers due to lack of clothes to fit me after all this activity and lack of food. They have made us swim every lake, canoe every river and climb trees, and do archery. ClimbMeister Gordon has told me I have a rare talent for archery, so if I disappear it's only because I

have absconded as Robin Hood. My life was not in vain.
Pleeeaze send food and lip-gloss (a pair of Diesel jeans size
26 would also come in handy).

Lots of love,

Lily XXX

I might as well beg some new jeans off Dad while he still
feels guilty about sending me away. If not now, when can
I? I want both Mum and Dad to know how hurt I am by
them clearly having booked this before they'd even
mentioned it to me. As though I'm an animal to be got
rid of. I don't hate it here, but it's weird being away for
the first time. Wanting things to be different at home
doesn't mean you want to be sent away.

Subject: Lovely Time

Dear Mum,

I hope you are having a lovely time with Mr Gill, sorry Adrien,
and Bay and Poppy. Please don't worry about me. I shall
survive somehow, foraging in the forest for bits of old nuts
and berries that have dropped off trees and sometimes out of
birds' poo. I think I ate the right red berries. It's only a little
stomach ache. Tomorrow we cross the desert on horseback.
It is renowned for its mercenary tribes, and if I am kidnapped
I will tell them not to shrink your and Dad's heads, but you
know warriors . . . you can't tell them anything.

We are going shopping for food this afternoon and if
I'm very good they might buy me a small carrot. Really, I

am so hungry I could eat your special burnt sausage and
bacon buttie.

But please don't worry about me.

Lots of Love,

Lily xxx

Nobel Prize for Chocolate

I send the e-mail off to Mum with a flourish of achievement. I feel it has just the right amount of suffering. I can't
make it as detailed as I'd hoped because Ann is gathering us
together to haul all twelve of us off in a minibus to go
shopping for the pony trekking trip tomorrow. We've each
been given money to buy our own supplies for two days. I
can already smell the chocolate soon to be burning a hole
though my pocket and burrowing a way into my stomach.
Chocolate is a lovely thing that should never be taken for
granted; it should be savoured with tiny little bites that
melt . . . I have to stop thinking about it. It's better to think
about chocolate than Maya, Belle and Izzy getting on
famously with Rose and Fiona, all knowing the same
sloaneypony brigade because they are all rich. I feel like I'm
in *The Outsider*, which is a book we read in reading club last
term by this great writer Albert Camus. Lonely we wander
in our existential internal deserts – like clouds, but so much
lonelier. That's why I've written so many e-mails.

And the boys. The boys. What is there to say? The less

the better. They have developed a gang mentality, like a pack of dogs, joining forces with the rest of the boys to sneer at the girls. Why are boys so damn immature? Sometimes I think that it is simply jealousy because we've got breasts and they haven't. Of course they have thingies that we don't, but who would want one of those (unless you've lost your pen and need to write your name in the snow with pee)? Just imagine the competition every time you have to go to a public urinal. Everyone's looking at yours and saying, 'Hmmm, not very big', or, 'Bad aim, old boy', or, 'Maybe you can find a very small person to marry'.

I would not want a thingy. Even fantasmagorically ridiculous bosoms are better than a front tail (the technical term, as used by scientists, Bea and me).

I am in DDM, having these great thoughts about humanity (expect to win the Nobel Peace Prize quite soon), when we are herded out of the bus like a mob of sheep and dumped in a supermarket.

'OK, you've heard what I said on the journey about nutrition, so go to it,' says Ann. I didn't catch any of that because I was in DDM, but she can't have said anything important.

I wander round the store alone (the others seem to go off to a different section) and fill my basket with the bare essentials:

Marshmallows
Toffee popcorn
Chocolate
Those really nice old-fashioned bottles of lemonade
Choc-chip cookies
Bubblegum
Chocolate cigarettes (for fun)
Supernoodles to keep Ann happy.

But when it comes to paying, I'm thirty-five pence short, so I have to make a saving and ditch the noodles.

Back at base, Ann goes through our purchases, and goes off on one when she sees what I have chosen.

Apparently, I have bought nothing but empty calories and can expect to starve. Like I'm going to believe that? How can they be empty? The chocolate alone has 2,000 calories. And when did they invent the day that I can't get full on chocolate and marshmallows?

The Marshmallow Meltdown

The boys are being stupid downstairs so Maya, Izzy, Belle and I come back upstairs to the dorm after the usual abysmal dinner.

'It's hard to think about the chickens that had to die for that,' I say, tummy still gnawing. 'They died in vain.'

'Why is it called Chicken Tango? I don't get it,' Belle asks.

'It was so busy dancing it forgot to be food?' I laugh.

'It was Chicken Marengo not tango, idiots,' Maya shouts.

'Who's in a bad mood?' comments Izzy.

Maya scowls. 'I want to go home. I can't stay here.'

'Ah, come on, Maya,' I say.

Maya starts crying, just soft little bleats at first. I feel awful. I want to cry too, and it's only the second day, with nineteen more to go. Belle, Izzy and me look at each other. There's a point when everything rests on a pinnacle, ready to tip over the edge and this is it. The edge can't be considered.

'That's it,' I say. 'Let's roast the marshmallows. Who's got matches?'

No one has.

'I've got a hairdryer,' suggests Belle.

The hairdryer's useless, all it does is blow the powder off and burn our hands. Izzy's hair straighteners are slightly better – the marshmallows go gooey and melty – but Iz is completely hysterical that we are ruining her ceramics. 'Stop!' she screams manically, but that's just Izzy being overdramatic as usual. I try not to let her annoy me, but I much prefer Belle.

'You'll turn my hair into burnt toffee.'

'Izzy, life is tough. You have to take chances, make sacrifices, for others to respect you. Don't be a wuss,' I tell her.

'I don't want your respect, I want my straighteners working. Do you know how much they cost?'

The alternative of putting the marshmallows on the hot water heater takes too long. Eventually I sneak over to the west wing and borrow some matches from the boys. On my return, I light an excellent fire in a metal bin. We begin to roast the marshmallows until we are interrupted by the fire alarm going off and Izzy shrieking.

'You mad pyromaniac! This is your fault!' Izzy is an A1 pain, landing me in it as Ann comes storming in with a fire extinguisher.

'I try to give people entertainment and this is the thanks I get?' I yell as I'm yanked out of the room by Ann.

But even being hauled off to the Prof's for a 'fire discussion' is worth it for the smile I see on Maya's face. She'll last another day at least.

The question is, after another confrontation with the Prof, will I?

CHAPTER FOUR
Ponies, Muck and Bums

Subject: My Will

Dear Bea,

Most odd. I sat up as fast as a slap in the face, wide awake and it's six a.m. *Vraiment!* So I'm writing to you. How are you, my little toenail clipping? I have already laid out everything on my bed, even packed my rucksack for the pony trekking trip today. I am being a good girl now because I almost got chucked out for burning marshmallows last night. Apparently I am a fire risk! Being prepared is odd and even enjoyable, instead of the usual home chaos, scrabbling for my socks or worse – Poppy's (and ones she's already worn. Yuck!).

I might just try this neat and tidy thing at home. Do you think there might just be something in it? A zillion grown-ups can't all be wrong can they?

Actually zillions of grown-ups are often wrong. When they are bombing the hell out of each other's countries, and busy starving each other to death, making grown-up mayhem into hell on earth for their own mad, greedy, tiny-minded ways. Have rethought tidiness. Am staying as was. You start going down one of those roads, and before you know it, you've turned into Hitler.

I opened a window as soon as I woke, and there was a big pink sky saying – Hey you, lovely, you might be the only one awake in the entire universe (not strictly true because there's probably someone out there fishing in the Outer Hebrides, doing things with sheep in Australia, or drinking blood from a cow in a Masai village in Africa) but I, the Big Pink Sky, am here happily covering you.

It's so beautiful, I want to smile and practise my special hoppity dance, which I am perfecting for whenever I become a rabbit, which, with the carrot/orange diet, might be quite soon. DO NOT repeat any of my sky thoughts to Mum. Otherwise, she'll be making me hug trees and talk to grass spirits, and I'd rather gabber to you.

It's weird, three days away and I'm beginning to really miss certain stuff. Obviously not the FishMan . . . Oh why do you have to be so annoying and not be here, Bea? I wouldn't have to talk to that stupid Izzy, who screamed at me when I melted marshmallow on her hair straighteners – honestly! I only put up with her because of her nice cousin Belle. If you were here we'd have such fun. You could come camping and ponytrekking, you'd like that wouldn't you? Of course you would. Only eighteen days to go, if I manage not to be eaten by bears, or mauled by escaped baboons. Pray for me.

Lots of Love,

Lily xxxxxxxxxxx

P.S. If I don't return I bequeath to you, Bea, My entire wardrobe, make-up collection and Billy obsession (you can have him anyway).

Maya's crying has kind of made me miss my family too. It's not like I miss Bay's potty in my bed, but Bay when he's cute, when he's all soft and sweet and not smelly – after a bath. Before he starts doing that kissy-farty thing on your face, and his nose bubbles with snot, and he's laughing so hard he wees all over the floor, or over you. The sweetie-cutie-pie. Or when he tries to wrestle you to the ground like he's some strong-man. Or when he believes you when you tell him his slippers are magic and fly round the room at night, keeping the monsters away. I love it when his eyes go all wide and his little gooey mouth drops down to dribble, and he's so excited he wiggles, saying, 'Yes? Yes?' like a sweet poggle.

Poppy. Now there must be something I miss about Popsicle? Oh yes, her clothes.

Mum I definitely miss. Just because she hugs me, whether I want it or not, whether my friends are around or not. She'll hug me and kiss me and say I am her 'Lil' bobble chicken', or that, 'You will always be my baby, no matter how big, podgy, ugly and old you get'. Which is reassuring in some ways, and not in so many others. I mean, you want your parents to believe in you, whether you turn into the prime minister or a postman, get big and podgy, or not. Obviously all Mum expects of me is that I am going to be big, fat, ugly and old. At least that's what she says in front of my friends. WARNING: don't mix adults and humour.

Mr Herrod in Science said that we are all made up of cells, that every living thing in the world is just different patterns and configurations of cells, but it's still all made from cells. It is hard to think that I am made from the same stuff as my dad, but there is clearly one exception – adult humour. How can I be made from the same stuff as that?

All I have to do is think of Dad and an e-mail from Suzi appears.

Subject: How camp? A little or very?

Dear Lily,

I knew you'd love the T-shirt, because you have such excellent taste: the same as mine. I am trying to separate your Dad from his wallet, which is a little like doing open heart surgery on a lion without anaesthetic or like trying to persuade him to go to a party. So I shall buy you the jeans, and send them to you tomorrow. I'm so jealous that you've managed to drop a whole size in a day?! People pay good money to get that thin, but I will include some food goodies too. And try to remember that lip-gloss is a cosmetic. You're not meant to eat it on toast, silly.

Have fun, wish I was there, honestly! Your dad's in one of his 'special' blue moods.

Love Suzi x

P.S. Can't quite see you as Robin Hood, but *Vogue* says that green tights are definitely back for autumn. I could see you in the mini tunic too, with matching hat, but would ask you to think again before you start growing a goatee beard – might put some of the boys off.

Suzi's e-mail makes me smile. Suzi is so great. And then I start to feel guilty. Poor Mum. I will read her e-mail and reply straight after writing to Suzi. Getting up early is quite good when you have this much time free.

Subject: Not very camp

Dear Suzi,

All goodies welcome in Sherwood Forest. Remember Robin Hood's saying when dealing with Dad's wallet: steal from the rich and give to the poor. I am poor, Dad is rich.

Am going off riding into the desert for many days. I will be especially hungry when I return because I have food with empty calories, apparently. Can you send parcel by fast post train rather than camel, please?

Merci, in bucket fulls.

Lots of love,

Lily xxx

P.S. I ate the mascara on toast, not the lip-gloss – that goes on ice cream, silly. Also don't think boys would notice if I had beard, moustache, or nose hair. Why are bosoms a different matter? What is it with boys and wet T-shirts?

Re: Lovely time
My Lil' Chicky,

Poppy read out your e-mail to me. I called your dad straight away about the desert. I thought you were going to the Lake District. If I'd known that's where your father was sending you, I'd have come too.

Dad just called and said that you are at Lake Coniston and that I shouldn't worry. You're getting on famously.

Bay is doing very well at talking. He said 'Adrien' yesterday. Poppy and I were thrilled.

As you say, I must not worry about you, though we all miss you. Adrien even said it seemed quiet without you around. It was nice of him to think about you.

I was going to send you five pounds but Adrien said you wouldn't really need it. Do you?

Can't wait for you to tell us about your exciting adventures.

Love you lots, big kiss,

Your Mum x

There is something so depressing about the e-mail from Mum that I can't answer it. It's like Adrien FishMan has stepped in and dragged his fishy fingers all over the e-mail, and replaced me at home. And what is Bay doing

64

saying 'Adrien'?! And Dad saying I'm getting on 'famously' – how does he know?

I decide to read Poppy's e-mail before I reply.

Subject: Mad Mother

Dear Sis,

Sorry about that last mad thing from the bonkers factory. I told Mum you'd want money and the finest of everything available to humanity, but adrien (no capital letters for his name. Should he have a name at all?) wanted to spend it on other women, drink and drugs. You know how men are. Anyway his fishfingers (boom boom) are all over the house. He seems to be staying here now and he's making me become a crazoid psycho bitch girl, I swear. He plays this music – argh! It's by a group called Yes. All I can say is, NO NO NO MORE!

I'm trying to do my important coursework and he tells me to go do it elsewhere. He's listening to Prog Rock, whatever that is? What I want to know is, whose house is it anyway? Am thinking of running away to Dad, but can't desert Bay, or can I now that he's said the alien's name? Mum's like, can't I be a bit nicer to the alien? The truth? No I can't. It is beyond me. Why did you have to go and have yourself replaced by the monster from outer space? Am doing extra shifts at the Chelsea Café just to escape home.

Suddenly I miss you. Did I say that? I know. Wish I were with you in happycamp hell. Might have a chance to do some work!

Love you, Flower.

Pops

Wow! Things must be bad if she's missing me. Poor
Poppy. I have thought of nice things to say about Poppy
at last. She is on my side, and in dark lighting she looks a
little like me, but she has a bum the size of a tiny mole. In
fact it is not even a bum, it's more of a *petit* yogurt pot,
which is a compliment coming from me.

Subject: HATE fishfingers

Dear Pops,

I'm sorry I have been replaced by alien lifeforce with fishfingers, not really my fault. Give the alien any drugs you can
find ground up in his tea, and let him be carted off to rehab.

I was missing home until I got your e-mail, thank you for
curing me. Let's call him 'argh' from now on. He needs to
be in an institution – his very own, not ours. This is what is
known as Care in the Community. He has brainwashed
Mum. Don't leave him alone with Bay – we must save the
children . . . even the trees.

Poor Pops, things must have got bad if you actually
want to work.

Flower Power Rules. Send chocolate.

Lots of love,

Lily xxx

P.S. He hasn't changed you into a 'crazoid psycho bitch' –
you're always like that before your period.

They are ringing the bell for breakfast and I am determined to get in first. My reply to Mum's e-mail will have to wait until I've recovered and got back from *Pony Madness – My Life as a Horse*. That's quite a good title for my memoirs. I know what everyone else's should be too:

My Life as an Evil Alien Lifeforce by A. Gill.
Tightwad – The Rules of Being a Dad by D. Lovitt.
Crazy as the Moon – Life as a Loon by J. Lovitt (Mum).
Baylife – Being a Tree by B. Lovitt
Genuis! My Sister Lily by P. Lovitt

I am so good at titles I think I shall be a professional titler when I'm old. I wonder if I'll need a job or just want one to escape the boredom of being so rich and famous?

I wonder if I will ever make it to a decent age before I die of family-related stress first, and lack of food?

The Fine Difference Between Muck and Poo

I have just eaten for breakfast two eggs, bacon, sausage (yes I should get the bravery award from Buckingham Palace, services to bad sausages) tomatoes, beans and toast. Two cups of tea with extra sugar and a glass of milk on cornflakes. I'm stocking up, considering how little I've had to survive on in recent times and knowing we'll be gone for a couple of days. Yes, standards drop drastically once you've forgotten what real food tastes like. I have forgotten.

I am thinking myself rather smart for my early morning manoeuvres, and I am alone at breakfast eating away (extra toast? Why, yes, thank you, my good man) when everyone rushes in at once, yelling, 'There you are, Lily! We've been looking all over for you.' 'We've called the police and your parents.' 'We thought you'd run away.' 'Your knapsack was gone.'

'What? I've already put it in the Land Rover for the trip. I only got up early. It may be unusual, but hardly a reason to call the police and have me arrested.'

'Honestly!' says Ann, as if I'd done something wrong. 'I suppose I'll have to call everyone up again and save your face, I mean say you're safe.'

'It might be an idea,' I reply.

'Sorry,' says Maya. 'My fault. When I saw you weren't in bed and your bag was gone, I assumed you'd skedaddled. After last night.'

'What about last night?'

'Well, you ruined my hair straighteners,' says Izzy.

'And set off the smoke alarms with the bin fire,' Belle adds.

'Hey, that was nothing. I'd completely forgotten about it. But if it makes you feel better, I ate all your *petits déjeuners*. I'm quite full.'

'Thank you, Lily, already the terrible guilt I was feeling has passed,' Maya jeers, and unnecessarily grabs at my last bit of toast.

'You can have that. I'm full,' I say.

'You are really selfless.'

Sick

Out at the stables I was beginning to regret my greed as Jumping Jackie was showing us how to muck out a stable.

'It's very interesting,' I say to her at the end. 'But why are you showing us?'

'Now it's your turn,' she replies, pointing at the shovels and other stinky stables.

It looked revolting, but that was nothing compared to the smell – it has me heaving my reconstituted breakfast into my throat. There is something particularly disgusting about swallowing sick, even your own. Imagine if you had to swallow other people's for a job? What do you do for a living? Oh, I'm a sick swallower.

I do the job in double quick time, just to get out of there. I thought I might have a chance to skive off afterwards, but Jackie hauls me back, enthusiastically showing everyone what a great job I have done. Apparently, I should feel proud – so proud that she gets me to do the one next door as well. Now that's what I call a reward! And then comes the grooming. Brushing your own hair might not seem much of a slog, but when you've got an entire horse covered in the stuff, there are easier ways to have fun.

* * *

'Have you ridden before? You've got a good seat,' Jackie says.

I don't tell her that I can't slump, even if my granny hadn't tied me to a broom handle when I was six (yes, she was as mad as my mother. Luckily it has bypassed me). I can't slump because of the huge bruise from banging my bum at the bottom of the banisters.

'It's easy. I can do horse stuff,' I say confidently. I went on a donkey in Spain once and it's all about clinging on, really.

'Do you want to hold the reins correctly and pull Lolly's head up from eating the grass, then?' Jackie asks.

'Like this,' Maya whispers to show me.

The rest of the morning seems to comprise of trying to stop Lolly eating, and clinging on for dear life every time he decides he wants to defy me and bite Blake's pony. That's bad enough, but then comes the trotting. Suddenly I know what it's like to be a woodpecker, but instead of your head it's your bum bumping up and down, and down and up again all on the bruised bit. When I thought I could take no more, the lunatic animal decides to race Maya's pony, Sherbert. So Sherbert and Lolly gallop like the contents of a sweet shop attached to a rocket, across the field, uphill, with Maya shouting,

'Lily, you all right? Do you want me to stop?'

Jackie is screaming, 'Stop those two!' as if we are robbers. To my surprise, when the panic passes I find myself enjoying it, shouting, '*Allez oop, je suis formidable, incroyable, magnifique!*' and other words of encouragement. Maya eventually stops, Lolly follows suit and, miracle of miracles, I stay on top and win. '*Tout les champignons!*' I say to Maya.

She isn't impressed. 'You might be a mushroom, but I am not.'

'You know what I mean. What's the French for champion, then?'

'There isn't one, frogs never win,' Blake adds, trotting up. 'Don't you know they just jump and croak. Ribbet ribbet'. He bulges his eyes at me unattractively, and William, coming up behind him, smirks. Boys! Are they really that stupid, or just trying to gain sympathy?

'It's *champion*,' said Maya.

'That's what I said,' I tell her.

Sad-witches and Warm Lemonade

At one o'clock we get off the horses and give them a rest by a stream while we eat lunch. I have a delicious meal of chocolate and marshmallows whilst everyone else has sensible things like fruit, cheese sad-witches (otherwise known as sandwiches to *les ordinaires*). The chocolate is a

71

perfect melty mush, *très magnifique avec les* marshmallows.

Afterwards, we ride for hours through the hills, the grass all dried out and burnt by the heat of early summer. God must have heard my prayers, and felt sorry for us with the sun beating down on our backs, because The Youth Lodge – a giant log cabin (*très rustique*) where we're staying overnight – backs onto a lake. We are so smelly and sweaty there is no way even Jackie wants to go near us, without our going in the water first. As we unsaddle and feed the ponies, both animals and boys are looking sniffily towards us girls and, considering how stinky animals and boys are . . .

We strip off to our swimsuits, which we'd put on under our clothes, and jump screaming into the cold, green lake, shaded by a cluster of weeping willows trailing their branches like fingers in the water. It's fun getting cold and water-bombing each other, before warming up again by lying on the dinosaur-grey rocks on the shore. The sky holds itself a cloudless blue before quickly turning cobalt as evening approaches. It looks like a poem of heaven. Poem of Heaven, did I invent that? I amaze myself some days. A light supper of chocolate and a warm lemonade, followed by a bed so hard and lumpy it's more like a rocky road, but I am too tired to notice. I figure sometimes life has to get better before it has a chance to get worse.

CHAPTER FIVE

Chocolate Pain
(Pain au Chocolat)

The relief of getting off a horse was so immense that even Base Camp seemed like a good idea. At least I was able to read Bea's e-mail and tell her everything that she was missing.

Subject: Cement Mixers

Dear Lilllllly,

My Bum is bigger than you think, but I reckon I have a way to get it back to Baci beauty. Small like a little choccy. Actually, 'baci' means 'kiss', as well as being an Italian chocolate, so – Baci my Bum! Quite funny. Ha ha ha. Is it the saddest thing in the world to cry alone? Or dance alone?

So yeah, I was searching through the cellar with Grandma trying to find her blender (for the making of essential peanut butter milkshakes – oh, it is a hard life) when I found this bunch of records and an old portable gramophone that looks like a picnic case. This thing is sooooo the best. And there are some mad records. It's all old jazz and used to belong to Gramps's mum's sister, who was, in his words, 'a Jazzbabe'.

Hey lil' Lil, let's be Jazzbabes when I get back? How cool will that be?

I don't know what they do but we can hang out being hip. Gramps says he's finding me a book all about Beatniks. Not quite sure what these are but will tell you when I find out. Anyway they used to listen to this mad crazy sound. There are songs about donuts and cement mixers, having big feet and pig foots and bottles of beer.

But my favorite is called Slim G – something or other. Just call me Slim, I like that.

Love,

Slim B.

Thank goodness for Bea. Bea makes me smile when even the worst of life is happening. Bea makes it possible for me to laugh in the face of my tragic existence, like my family and all the other animals here. Bea even makes me laugh at myself when I'm sore, sick and tired and exaggerating.

Subject: Beat Nik? What's he ever done to you?

Dear Slim B good,

Oh my God. Pain like you have never known. Two (but it felt like three) days sitting on a horse and my bum is sorer than any sore ever felt, in the worst sores of humanity. If childbirth is as bad as this I am going to make sure I'm neutered like your cat. How do cowboys do it? I mean ride all day long! Do they have special bottom pads? Can you ask one for me? I always thought I had special bottom pads – bum fat – but they are not doing their job. I am having to sit on five pillows to write this.

I am also sick – no, not in the mind. It's worse than that. I will never taste a Baci. Writing this is v. hard. I never thought it would come to this, but I AM SICK OF CHOCOLATE. Official. After two days of only melted chocs and marshmallows and warm, flat lemonade, all frying in the heat, I'll probably never eat sugar again. Not even at Christmas. I don't think I'll even be able to watch *Charlie and the Chocolate Factory* again. Just thinking of the chocolate river makes me *très malade*. Cancel all choc gifts. Sorry. How will the chocolate trade survive without me?

Je n'aime pas, le chocolat.

Could this be the beginning of Beatnik poetry?

I am a Jazzbabe as I already love Billie Holiday. Don't you remember the foggy day song, about losing the British Museum? Very careless!

Your Lily of the Chocolate Vomitorium x

I couldn't tell her, I didn't want to admit how miserable I really was. I thought I could tell Mum, but Mum just plain makes me want to scream.

Subject: Are you all right

Dear Lily,

Are you all right? You haven't replied to me. I was worried
after you didn't run away (they called me to say you
hadn't). Poppy says I must send you food as you are
starving. You did sound hungry in your e-mail, so I've sent
some chocolate biscuits and a few favs of yours. What kind
of place is this? I tried to speak to the Professor, but all he
kept on saying was that he'd have a discussion with you
when you returned. Odd man. Where have you been?

Anyway, I expect you are enjoying yourself despite the
conditions, so don't worry, I'm not worrying about you.

Have to go, Adrien's made supper for us all. What a treat.

All my love,

Mum x

After reading her e-mail I didn't just want to scream, I
wanted to rub her face in the dirty nappy of my pain. I set
to work to make her feel really sorry for me.

Subject: Alive

Dear Mum,

I am alive, just about. They have had us working night and
day, cleaning out horses' poo and riding for nineteen hours
a day. I am very tired and sore, and the beds are as lumpy
as your mashed potatoes. I expect they'll want me to go
and dig the garden or clean the windows or lick the bins.
You did say they were paying Dad, didn't you? The beating

doesn't hurt too much, though my bum is still very sore, black and blue. They say the damage is not permanent, but emotionally I can't be sure. I think you can see therapists at the doctors, so it won't cost you too much.

Anyway, thank you for thinking of me, please no more chocolate, they've turned me against it. Have a lovely dinner.

Is it pie? Steak and kidney pie with gravy, mash and green beans, hot apple crumble for pudding with cold vanilla ice cream? I can but dream, oh and how I dream.
Love,
Lily xxx

I thought I had succeeded, but I read Poppy's e-mail and then realised there is no getting through to Mum.

Subject: THE MUM
Dear Lily,
She's being weird again. I don't like it. Tell her to stop, Lily. Remember when Dad left and Mum started cleaning and throwing everything out? She's doing that again.

I have a horrible feeling she's making space for the argh! She sends Bay and me to bed at the same time – of course I tell her she's mad and that I do what I want in my house, so they storm out and leave me to babysit Bay.

Last night they came back stinking of pubs and shouting, waking us up. Do they have no self control? That's what I asked. 'Oh stop being such a prudey prune,' was Mum's adult reply, while argh asked if I wanted a drink! I slammed my door in disgust. Come home Lil, all is forgiven.

Love

Poppy x

Subject: Demented Adults

Dear Poppy, Poor Poppy,

Ignore them. At least you can, but my bum's hurting so much I can't ignore it, at least they aren't attached to you, like said bum. Sorry I didn't write for a few days, but playing at cowboys takes time.

What can I say about this place that will make you feel any better about home? I spent yesterday in cold, damp clothes because I forgot to pack jeans and T-shirts. The trousers I had on were pretty rank and too thin, so all the insides of my thighs are lovely and chapped.

Then I got sunstroke and was shouted at by a leader. Everyone was being nasty to me, including my friend Maya, laughing as I got made an example of by JumpMeister Jackie, who practically put me on a baby lead, all the way back, for forgetting my hat. I'm sure being tied to a rose bush and beaten by birch sticks would have been kinder. The one thing that's good is that you are so tired at the end of the day all you want is a cold shower and bed. Most nights I am too tired to shower, so I also smell rank now.

Being smelly has affected my brain. I can't even think properly to help you. All I can suggest is trip-wire, strung higher than Bay. Put the mad cases all in hospital with broken legs and then you'd have the house to yourself. Yourself and Bay.

Hey, swimming races this afternoon – at least I can do that and I won't have to walk, or sit. Looking forward to a delicious lunch of yesterday's grated cheese and carrot salad on ready wilted lettuce with no dressing, and some delicious, greenish pickled egg with no mayo, salt or pepper.
Chin up, Popsy, you could be here.
Lots of love,
Lily x
P.S. Am doing brilliantly at being told off for 'excelling in improprieties', whatever they are? Another thing I'm good at!

Why does everything have to change? There I was, happy, winning the pony race and, I don't know – I mean, I'm not sure what happened. I'd like to blame the planets, but JumpMeister Jackie is determined to blame me for 'playing the clown' and endangering my own safety. It felt like somebody had decided that the rest of the trip was 'be mean to Lily' time. It felt like everything I did was wrong. Trouble became my shadow. I am sent to see the Prof as soon as we are back.

I sat in his study and waited as he stared at me and didn't blink. Ever. For the first time I realised how small he was – the image of a garden gnome came into my head and I couldn't get it out.

'Why are you so, so, so, upset that you have to keep on

upsetting everyone else around you?' he asked. He has this weird voice that goes very high when he gets excited and very low when he's serious. I find it hard not to laugh when he sounds so silly.

'I don't think I am upset,' I said.

'You are. Believe me you are,' he countered.

'I'm only upsetting the leaders.'

'You might have failed to notice, but they are human beings too.'

He was right. I hadn't realised the leaders were human.

'Lily. Why do you feel this compulsion to take over and talk all the time without letting anyone else get a word or thought . . .' And so he mashed on and on, doing just what he'd told me off for doing.

This is surely, to borrow Mum's favourite saying, the pot calling the kettle black, but something told me to keep my mouth shut. What is it with little men? Napoleon was small and bossy. Is that a coincidence? Imagine being a man and being really little, and having fish hands. What would it be like? Like being Adrien FishMan from the wine bar.

'So am I free to go?' I asked at the end of the drone, when he was back to doing the weird staring thing.

'Yes, Lily, but with a warning.'

I took my warning like a man (do men take things differently from girls?) and came straight down here to the computers to collect and write e-mails.

Thank God for e-mail (one of His greatest inventions), along with boys, Paris and music. And thank God for Bea, who must have been on the Internet; as I sent Poppy's reply I received this:

Subject: Chocoholics Anonymous

Dear Lily,

This is the best thing that could have happened to you. Halleluja ha ha. Nobody wanted to tell you, but everybody's been really, well, how do I say this, concerned about your relationship with chocolate. When you started deserting your friends because you'd rather hang with a bar of Fruit and Nut and talk to the wrapper, we knew something was wrong. Surely there is more to life than chocolate?

Right now, as I bite into a pale white Cookies and Cream Hershey bar, I don't know what that is, but you're my friend and I'm glad you've found out. It's a safer place for someone like you with such deep, sweet problems, right? Wrong, so wrong.

If you can't even watch *Charlie and the Choc***** Factory*, you are a total . . . LOSER. I thought you had more stamina than to give up after only two days – WUSS. It's nothing to be proud of, think of all the poor cocoa farmers you'll be depriving of a livelihood. Some are children. Don't be so selfish. None of us like chocolate. It's not just all about You You You. It's also about your (once upon a time) good friend. I'm not saying that our friendship is conditional, but I think we both know it is where the ch**'s concerned.

Be gone. And no kisses until you shape up think about Bay – what will he do if you don't share your choc***** with him anymore?

Farewell Ratfink . . . Until you've learned to love (the sweet smell of choc*****) again.

Slim B

Oh, what would I be without Bea as a friend? Probably quite thin. I thought it was me with the chocolate obsession, but I'm starting to suspect she's a pusher and likes it even more than I did. The unfair thing is she always remains so skinny and unspotty, no matter what she eats. I love Bea, but that doesn't make it fair.

CHAPTER SIX

The Best Medicine

Laugh? I almost died.

'Have you got your swimsuit on already?' Maya says, sprinting into the Common Room.

'No.' We have swapped roles. I am now the misery. Unhappiness has a way of washing over you like a wave and I have no control, or as much as I would over a hurricane.

'What's eating you?'

'Nothing. I just . . . ache.'

'Why didn't you do the tree climbing this morning? It was great – we made a tree house.'

'I . . . I had emails to write.'

The truth is I don't know what to say after the pony trek. Everything changed when everyone laughed at me like I was some idiot. I want everybody to like me, but I feel as twisted as Play-Doh in five different colours, all confused into one. I want to be alone, like some tragic misunderstood movie star, but am annoyed when everyone leaves me for two hours sitting all by myself typing e-mails. My head hurts and when I walk it's like Lolly is still between my legs, an attractive bow-leg look not compatible with any known fashion. No wonder cowboys walk so strangely.

'You can't spend all day in here. Come on, Lily. Anyway, it's lunchtime and there'll be nothing left.'

I allow Maya to drag me down the corridor to the delights of the orange and grey canteen. It's so ugly and sterile that I miss our muddled family kitchen, crowded with Mum's plants and avocado-growing experiments. OK, so it looks like a greenhouse in Kew Gardens, but at least it has life, even if all the food comes out of it burnt to death.

Maya was right, there is nothing decent left except one cheesy baked potato. I make a grab at the exact time as William. Our fingers meet, and then our eyes. One of those terrible moments of pleasure-whipped embarrassment.

'I, I'm sorry – you have it.'

It's the first time I've heard his voice, and it's soft, shy and low (it isn't a shrieking, helium aberration!). He also has eyelashes that I could only achieve with a vat of mascara.

'No, you got there first.'

'I didn't really want it.'

'Are you sure?'

'Yes, you have it. Honestly.'

'If no one's going to make up their minds, I'll have it.'

Blake grabs the potato. I should be angry, and William too, but instead we do the oddest thing: we start laughing. And once we start we can't stop, because every time we look at each other it starts all over again. What on earth are we laughing about? Neither of us knows, but the way everyone else is looking at us like loons certainly helps.

Ann finally tries to break it up, but laughter like that, once it starts, is as hard to stop as a bike without brakes that's hurtling down a roller coaster. When I sit down to eat I don't even care that I'm eating yesterday's cheese salad, I can't remember. William and I are put at furthest parts of the room from each other, but just one of his looks starts me off all over again.

'Can't you two shut up?' Blake shouts angrily, which of course is the wrong thing to say. His severe tone makes everyone else catch the laughter virus. We are soon all helpless, lying on the floor, Maya and me rolling about like worms in the grass. The leaders give up, the manic laughter vibe is too strong.

It's me who stops first. I have run dry. I wipe the tears away, take a deep shuddering breath and sigh, exhaling every giggle in my shaking body. I go upstairs to change into my bikini, and I can't feel one bit of pain. Laughing is such a miracle.

I am a genius. The magic cure for everything is laughter. How can I market it as a cure for all pain and aches? William and I had laughing hysteria and now I feel so well I could probably eat chocolate. Once we're married and I am a famous scientist with such a major discovery, would I have to use my married name? I could just give him a dedication, couldn't I?

I'll put decisions to one side, go swimming and swoon over William. There is one big problem with him, though. He wears boxer shorts that have Father Christmas dancing with his reindeer. You can see the waistband. Neither seasonal nor swimwear.

Do boys really not notice these things? If there's one thing I can teach Bay, it's that sex machines have to dress the part. As Bay's just a herb, it's not relevant. Still, any girlfriend of Bay's – once he learns that you don't drag your potty around in civilised society – will be proud to be seen with him, he'll be so perfectly styled by me. It's a duty to be performed for the sisterhood of all girls when you have a brother. In the same way you hope that a boy you go out with won't tuck a golf jumper into their trousers on your first date. If William's got a sister, she doesn't understand this.

A Bigger Splash

Splash! Dive, twist, somersault, backward somersault, butterfly . . . If there's one thing I was made for, it was water. I suspect that in another life I might have been a dolphin.

All is perfect, the sun in a cloudless sky, and I am

happy again, how is that? . . . Until I dive in. And as my bottoms come down, yes, my top comes off. *Pourquoi moi?* I don't have time to even consider the coldness of the water. One arm struggles to cover my bra area while the other tries to haul up my bikini pants. I think I've managed, until Maya starts pointing maniacally, and not only do William and Blake begin to laugh, but every other boy gathers to see my Lily pads floating. I grab the top, take a deep breath and sink lower than I feel. I rearrange my buzzwams and return to the surface, where Jackie is shouting 'Lily' and prodding a pole into the lake.

'I'm here. What's wrong?'

'Is it your aim to give everyone heart attacks? You disappeared under the water for ages. Don't do it again!' She gives me a steely stare before continuing. 'Now, is everyone ready for the marathon swim across the lake? I will be in the water with you, if there's any trouble, and Ann will be in the boat too. So Lily, try to keep close to Ann just in case. OK?'

How can I tell her my ambition is to swim the Channel, but, having a serious aversion to rubbing myself with duck fat, I've only ever swum the distance in my local swimming baths for a charity swim?

'On your marks, get set, GO!' Jackie yells. And off I go like a demon warrior, slicing through the dark water of Lake Coniston as if it is my enemy to be cut down. I keep going, the wind blowing small waves into my face, but still I'm easily at pace with the boys. But right in the middle a cloud covers the sun and it gets so freezing I want to pee. Unfortunately, Blake is right next to me, so I bite inside my lip until the feeling passes. However, I have to slow down for what seems like forever, and that is when Jackie passes me. I get back out in front though, and Blake takes it in turns with me to lead. But just as we near the end, suddenly Jackie jumps out of the water and announces herself the winner.

'Well done, guys, but I think I just beat you.'

Was it supposed to be a race against leaders?

Blake is second, and I'm third. But I'm not going to be beaten. I'm a bad loser when it comes to swimming. I start swimming back to the centre, and William and Blake start swimming after me, gaining fast. I am a machine – a swimming machine. I can hear Jackie getting in a state, and the boys trailing behind, so when I am quite sure that no one is around, I let go and pee my legs warm, like deep sea divers do in their wet suits (which is far more disgusting than peeing into a huge lake like Coniston). Then I keep swimming, even when I hear Jackie shouting that it is too dangerous to swim so far in one day, that it is only a one-way race. I swim and swim, arms crawling over my head, face down in – urgh. I wonder how many other people have peed in this lake? But my arms and legs are kicking, like Bay in a strop. At the other end I am so exhausted I can hardly stand up. William and Blake arrive a little later, out of breath and swearing. When the others are back on the same shore – thanks to Ann's boat – everyone cheers at my long-distance stunt. Maya suggests the boys carry me like a trophy hero on their backs, but since they can hardly walk either we stumble along until the heavens open and once again we are as wet as fish.

'You're obviously a strong swimmer, Lily. That was a very long swim indeed,' Jackie says.

'Oh, that's a quarter of what I usually do, when I'm in the Channel,' I say, and wink at Maya.

Crazy Like a Loon

Twenty of us slump in front of the telly, fighting for sofa space and the last beanbag. Rain has stopped play. A few boys are arguing over the pool table, and I can tell the leaders are delighted to have an afternoon off. They probably do rain dances when they're not with us. Outside there is an impressive display of thunderclaps and, on the telly, *My Parents Are Aliens*. Trying to keep warm, we put hot water into not nice squash and dunk not Nice biscuits. We are all a little gloomy, cooped up inside. There is something about grey summer rain . . .

'That mum and dad are so not weird, even for aliens,' I comment.

'Lily, most parents don't go invisible,' Izzy says seriously.

'Mine do,' said Belle.

'Yes, yours do, don't they?' agrees Izzy, as though it's an interesting truth, rather than just bizarre.

'Why's the dad so gay? He is so gay,' says William, helpfully.

'My dad's gay,' says Maya. Everybody stares. 'What? He is. He carries a handbag.'

'Well, most parents don't go crazy, do they?' Ian says sensibly.

'Mine do,' I say.

'What's the craziest thing your mum has ever done then?' asks Blake.

'Ah, that's easy. It was when my dad left us and moved in with his twenty-two-year-old secretary called Suzi, who, as my mum says, "is young enough to be your daughter, you dirty old man!" Mum was quite angry about it. She drove his car through their living room window.'

I imagine that everyone's faces go blank at this because it isn't crazy enough, so I tell them about the tree hugging, and how Mum called my baby brother Bay because she wants him to be strong and flavoursome. To make it funnier, I add, 'And to put in stews. One day she even chopped up all the chairs for the fire and we don't even have a fireplace.'

I am making myself laugh quite a lot with the memory,

because it all seems so silly. I'm sure one of the others is going to say, 'That's nothing, my mum's stripped naked and kissed the prime minister,' or whatever crazy things other parents do.

But all of them seem to agree that what my mum did beats their parents hands down; there is no competition. Which is depressing. Athough *I* know Mum is crazy, I don't necessarily want everyone else to agree. Saying it out loud also has the strange quality of making it sound more crazy and more real than I usually think it is. Still, everyone is very nice to me for the rest of the day, and lets me have first choice at the canteen. Some even say I am the best and fastest swimmer in the entire world – not quite true when you watch the Olympics. 'And at least you aren't ugly,' Blake says.

'And that's a compliment? You weirdo,' says Maya. 'You're supposed to say girls are beautiful.'

'Yeah, right. When I see one that is I'll tell her, but surrounded by mingers it's quite hard.'

Understandably we all have to jump on Blake and beat him.

In the mayhem, William leans over to me and whispers that he thinks I am the prettiest girl in the camp, and he offers me his last piece of gum. Maybe it is worth having a crazy Mum, just to have William tell me that and smile.

CHAPTER SEVEN
Levels of Madness

'Are you water-mad?' asks Blake as we walk through a dripping glade, pale green with light filtering through the leaves. The rain has stopped another morning climb, much to ClimbMeister's upset. So we are doing a forest walk instead.

'I think it's just normal, average madness. Nothing special,' I tell him.

'She is a fish,' Maya says.

'I am a fish.' I do my finest goldfish impression. 'Or I could be an otter?'

'Is it better to be an otter than a fish?' William shyly interrupts on the other side of me.

'I think they might be nobler,' I say, catching his eye. 'Otters, I mean.'

I stop caring about the conversation because I'm happily slipping into DDM. I was starting to think that

William might be better than any poster on my wall. He smiled at me over bad porridge this morning, and has now asked if it is better to be an otter than a fish. He is obviously a deep thinker, a good-looking brain box. In my family of animals, one of us has to improve our DNA's chance of survival.

'Of course it's better to be an otter than a fish. Are you stupid or something?' Blake rants at William, bringing me back to reality. 'Otters eat fish for breakfast, lunch and dinner – or hadn't you noticed, Eeyore?'

'Yeah, I suppose they do.' William smiles goofily at me.

He's sweet. Unlike Blake, who is having a spitting competition with Maya, while showing off, jumping up into trees with Ian, Tony and Ben, unnoticed by ClimbMeister who Sam, Rosie and Fiona are sucking up to.

'I think it would nice to be a beautiful, you know, exotic fish in a tropical lagoon,' Izzy says, giggling. 'Then you could swim every day in the sun by white sand beaches. Don't you think, Will?'

'Yes, that would be nice,' he replies.

NICE, NICE? What did 'nice' actually mean??? And was it nice that William was smiling at Izzy calling him Will? There is something so horrible about real people and the way they behave in real life, as opposed to posters.

'If I were an animal, I'd be a cat,' I say. 'What would you be Izzy, my dinner?'

'No, silly, if I was an animal I'd be a really sweet cocker spaniel with droopy ears.' Her voice sinks into baby talk. Yuck. I don't mind Bay doing baby talk, but he's a baby. Actually, sometimes it really annoys me, and HE is a baby.

'At least you wouldn't need surgery for that,' I almost say, but stop myself, which proves how mature I am. Izzy is getting on my nerves. I hate the way she pretends to be so dumb, blonde and helpless, so that she can get boys to do stuff for her. I also hate that Belle, who is far nicer, and with browner hair, sticks up for her because they are cousins. I even hate Izzy for having a small bottom, and very long legs, and being really pretty. Usually only Poppy irritates me in that way. Apart from their devious shifty smugness, they aren't that similar. Poppy is nicer than Izzy because, well . . . because she's my sister. Poppy might tease me remorselessly, but she doesn't and wouldn't flirt with my crushes, probably because they're too young for her. But still the point is she doesn't do it and one has to be grateful for small mercies.

'Hey, can anyone hear that noise?' asks Belle.

There's a definite sound of rushing water. We come out from under the trees into a clearing, and the most beautiful waterfall is in front of us, with a rainbow painted across it. Only a unicorn and fairies are missing from the picture.

'Wow,' we all say at once, and laugh.

'I'm there first.' Blake tears off his clothes, runs up to grab a branch and Tarzans his way in, slipping and hitting the ground awkwardly. Everyone laughs, but I can see that it hurt.

'Ouch! You poor thing. Are you all right, Blake? Let me see,' I say.

'Look, it's nothing,' he replies tersely. He's so irritable.

'You've got a massive graze. Do you want to go back and have it seen to?'

'I'm not a bloody baby. And since when were you Florence Nightingale?'

'OK, OK, I was only trying . . .'

'Well, don't.'

That is the last time I am going to help any boy. I am sticking to posters from now on. I jump in the water in my swimsuit. The sound of the falls fills my ears as I float down in the fizz of bubbling water. Is this what bathing in champagne would be like? We just need the gentle pop of bottles being opened.

'Let's see if we can get behind the actual falls,' Izzy giggles, climbing out of the water with her tiny bum, in her itsy microdot bikini. She's like a mosquito on a perfect day, something you just want to slap quiet.

'William? I bet you can't catch me,' she says, heading towards the waterfall.

95

'Hey! None of that running, we don't want any accidents,' says ClimbMeister from behind a newspaper, sitting on a nearby rock.

'No thanks, I want to swim.' William smiles at me, as though he knows I am cross and is trying to make peace.

As he swims towards me, a voice shatters our romantic moment. 'HELP!' screams Belle. 'Izzy's fallen under the fall – she's disappeared!'

William dives under the water, quickly followed by Blake, Ian, Ben and Tony. William surfaces with a lifeless Izzy in his arms, and swims to the side. We all pull her up the bank. William starts to put her in the recovery position, while the ClimbMeister appears and just watches. It is only when William's mouth touches Izzy's that I see her smile, her eyes batting behind their closed lids. I realize the whole thing is a complete stunt.

'Maya, look at the way she's putting her arms around his neck. She looks suspiciously alive. Drowning! My cat!'

'Dirty cow. It's the only way she could kiss him,' Maya points out.

'Actually, I asked Izzy to do that as part of your rescue practice,' says ClimbMeister. 'Thank you, Izzy. William that was very good.'

'Poor William,' I say.

'What do you mean "poor William"?' Blake joins in. 'Nobody offered me a kiss and my back's still sore!'

We jump back in the water playing aquatic kiss chase, while Izzy pretends to recover. How dumb is William to fall for that? Blake's so much funnier and smarter, most of the time, when he's not being mean.

Homesick Blues

'I want to go home,' Maya moans.

'You can't go home yet – we've just started having fun,' I say to her. 'And we've only been here a week.'

'It's not you. You and Belle are fun. I just want to be back home.'

I have to think quick. It would be terrible if Maya left me with just Belle and Izzy. After all, they are cousins and blood is thicker than water, and they'd end up thicker than thieves. And there are still two weeks to go. I would be alone with Rosie and Fiona in our group plus Ian, Tony and Sam. And I didn't know anyone in the other two groups.

'You can't go. The first midnight fancy dress feast is tonight,' I tell her quickly.

'Really? What feast? Nobody told me. You've made it up.'

I had caught her. 'That's because every night there's a secret – from tonight to the end. One person knows and has to plan it as a surprise with one other person for everyone else in their group. I don't know about the rest of the week but tonight is definitely the fancy dress midnight feast. You have to stay.' I was making it up as I went along. 'Please say you'll stay.'

'My dad's picking me up tomorrow. I called him this morning.'

'*Absolument pas!* Cancel him. Say you've changed your mind.'

'Lily, I want to go home. Not because of him . . . I miss Meg. I know that sounds odd, but she's always with me. I miss her and my things so much I feel sick.'

'That's just the food. We all feel like that.'

'Oh Lily, but . . .'

'It'll be so boringly *ennuyeux* with no you. Nothing *intéressant*.'

'Hey, why don't you come and stay with me back in London?'

'But I already live in London.'

'Ok, you could come and stay with us in France. We've got a place in Biarritz. It's really cool, a huge villa right by the beach. You can be as pretentious as you like with your French.'

'Pretentious? *Moi?* Well, I *do* have to practise before I move to Paris. *Vive la France!*'

'God, my parents will probably want to adopt you.'

'Maybe we can do an exchange. I'll go and live in your house in Chelsea and you can live in Battersea. If I can still visit my granny in France.'

'OK. Where's Battersea?'

'Maya, it's across the river from you!'

'I meant where in Battersea?'

'Oh right, by the park.'

'Look, I don't want to be boring and have to leave, but . . .'

I could sense that what Maya was trying to explain was too hard for her to tell. So I interrupt. I don't like to see her struggling. Friends don't need to know everything. And when it's that hard for a friend, you just have to try to make things easier. It seemed odd to me that she was missing her Nanny Meg more than her mum, but it was more proof of this mixed up, shook up world.

'Me neither. Let's never be boring and mad like our parents!'

'Pact.'

'Pact.'

Izzy walks into the dorm and slumps on her bed. We move on to talking about our plans for life, love and world domination. After five minutes of us ignoring her (because of her kissing stunt with William) she says, 'Oh yeah, there's a parcel for you downstairs.'

Maya and I don't wait to find out which of us. We run down the stairs so fast we knock into the Prof. What is the point of him? Other than promoting beard growth?

'Hello, Professor. We are looking for the parcel,' we say.

'Yes?'

'It's for me,' we say together, and burst out laughing.

'I'm not sure it's for both of you, but we'll see.' He disappears and comes back with two parcels, both for me, and a letter for Maya. Then he smiles.

Alors! From the wrapping I know who has sent what. The one beautifully wrapped in 1950s beefcake body-guards in leopardskin Speedos, holding bunnygirls like trays in their hands, could only have come from Suzi. The rumpled brown paper one – or 'recycled', as she calls it – is clearly from Mum. I know recycling is better, I know we use up too much of the world's resources on useless things but . . . I can't help but prefer Suzi's to Mum's eco-warrior wrapping. I don't want to, I want to prefer my mum's but sometimes life just makes it so difficult.

'Wow! Who are they from?' asks Maya as we go back upstairs. 'Mine's just boring money from Mum.'

'*L'argent, Maya, n'est jamais ennuyeux.* It's not the money, it's the way that you spend it. Mine are from Mum and Dad. Dad's hopeless at wrapping,' I lie to cover my mum's scrappy packing. I know it's a lie, but nice lies don't count as lies, if they're not vindictive.

Back in the dorm, I tear open Suzi's package, and out tumble a pair of the best jeans, a little tight, but I could just squeeze into them if I lie down on the floor to do them up. Stuffed in the pockets are an assortment of lip-gloss and eyeliner in different colours, some chocolate and bubblegum, with a card: *Have fun, love Suzi X*. Dad might have squiggled a signature but it was hard to tell. It could have been the cat's paw print. I hide the card.

Mum's has a whole letter, a box full of biscuits, sachets of Swiss hot chocolate, squirty cream, waffles and, between the dried fruit snacks, a secretly hidden fiver.

Dear Lily,
Hope you are having a lovely time darling, and haven't broken your leg (or anybody else's) yet! We all miss you like mad. Bay wanders round the house saying, 'Lily, where Lily?' and won't come out of your room without the bribe of at least a banana at bedtime. Poppy is very quiet, getting on with her work and the café. The house is strange without you.
The good news is one of Adrien's friends has offered me an exhibition after seeing some of my old paintings, so I've been popping into the studio and de-rusting my paint brushes. I'm quite excited.
Anyway, we all miss and love you, but you know that. Food is to make sure you come back alive.
All our love,
Your old Mum x
P.T.O. – from Bay to Lily.

On the back is a typical Bay work of art, alien style. A huge squiggle of paint. I think he's trying to paint a big smiley face and a stick body. Poppy's obviously helped him.

I don't know why, but I have to bite my cheek to stop myself crying, gulp down the lump stuck in my throat and blink until the tears disperse.

'Are you all right?' Maya asks quietly.

'Yeah, of course, Maya. Hey,' I sniff, 'at least we've got stuff for the midnight feast.'

'You are so lucky to have divorced parents,' says Izzy. God, I want to hit her.

'Your mum must be so cool to send you these jeans,' Belle adds. 'What's this about a midnight feast?'

'Yeah, she is. She really is.' I pull myself together, pretend to sneeze, blow my nose. I miss my mum, I really do. I'm sure Suzi would understand. I cross my fingers behind my back. 'Now, this midnight feast. What else do we need?'

'Fancy dress,' says Maya.

'Oh, we can just make that up. Dress up in each other's stuff,' I reply. Maya and I reveal the plan.

'What about tarts?' says Belle.

'I think we've got quite enough of those in this room,' says Maya, back in the spin of it. I hide my resentment towards Izzy in the spirit of world peace and partying. I am really far more mature than even I ever realised. Together we write a shopping list of what we want, make a lucky dip dressing-up box of weird bits of clothes, and pool our make-up for later on. Until called for our next activity, it's just work, work, work!

After our afternoon activity of practising camping – putting up tents and pulling them down – I finally get to sit down and write to Bea.

Subject: Boo!
Dear Bea is for a beautiful, brilliant, brainy blingthing.

Sorry I have been slow writing, but you know my brain (and if you don't, no one else does). Getting into the swing of camp fun by stealing bicycles and riding away from playing football on a mud-logged field.

We cycled to the village which is the weirdest place. You expect it all to be very Ye Olde Country. Not at all. Maya (you'll have to meet her) renamed it SloaneSquaresdale. Everyone has green wellies and red cords and jeeps.

Planning big fancy dress midnight feast. Food glorious food. I never thought I would look forward to a sausage roll quite so much. Ya-boo-sucks to your buckets of milkshake or whatever keeps you alive.

The mighty Lily (Queen of All the Woodland) has returned (and mightier than before. Me thinks captain!).

While I am at the computer, before high tea and before inventing my fabulous costume, I get in my thank yous.

Parents and other grown-ups think these are a very big deal, and I have noticed that the sooner you say thank you, the happier they are. Plus Mum did give me some money and that's always worth a thanks – you never know when it might happen again!

Subject: Package
Dear Suzi
Thank thank thank you you you – thanks.
   I love love love them. In French – *Amour, amour,* I want some more.
Lots of love,
The Queen Poet Lilyete x
P.S. This is modern poetry. Appreciate. I don't expect Dad will.

Subject: Package
Dear Mum,
Thank you. I just got the package it was all so sweet, (don't know how I can tell, I haven't eaten it all yet). Kiss Bay, and tell him he is a squadge button. Better than Picasso (he must get it from you) and thank you for the money. And give Poppy a hug too.
   I do miss you all. Busy organising party, write soon.
Thanks for everything . . .
Lots of love,
Lily x big hug xxxxx

And just as I send this off, up pops this from Poppy. Her ears must have been burning.

Subject: Trip-wire

Dear Lily,

The argh has disappeared for several days into his bacteria den. Mum has disappeared into her studio, at the bottom of the garden, and Bay is sitting on his potty next to me, smiling and saying 'Lily?' 50 million times. It's because I told him I was writing to you. The first time was cute. Now, quite dull. How can something look so sweet, but smell like a skunk?

Hope you liked goodies I chose. Dried fruit – Mum's idea to keep you 'regular'!

I am still obsessed by fishman – he winds me up like an elastic band airplane. He doesn't realise he is a member of a subspecies, which is funny when he tells me how to use a knife and fork, or anyone else what to do. Why does he think he's qualified when he's a visiting alien?

Yesterday, I listened to him tell four people what to do about their car, dinner, child, job, love life. If the aliens don't reclaim him, or drop an asteroid on his head, some other lifeforce wandering out of the Duck pub will.

Have fun. Oh Bay, did you have to? Yes, it's another miracle poo-bum to clean up.

What can you do? I know what Bay can do, and not much else. Best just call him Poo.

Love Pops x

CHAPTER EIGHT

Whose Life Is This Anyway?

Subject: PONDLIFE

Jazzbabe

Hey Lily, wake up! So it's 4 in the morning for you, so what!

So what happened last night with the party? Snog any boys? Did you know that French for kissing is *baiser*, but that it can also mean doing it! I was looking in my gramp's dictionaries. So I hope you didn't *baiser* anyone, ha ha. If you did, it should have been a *bisou* or *embrasse* which is a bit like embarrass, and knowing you, you were very embarrassing.

I actually saw a boy in the street yesterday and he was cute. Drop dead dreamboat. A fully automated Buff Being. You aren't the only one with boys, girl.

Did you snog? Should we have a kissing or *bisou*-ing competition? No, not together, you disgusting lezzy.

You've got the head start, as in you've talked to them (if

they truly exist – you might have made them up just to
make me jealous and I'd never know), but then I am a lot
prettier than you . . . I'll obviously beat you hands down
and it's not even my fault. Put it down to good genes – I've
got them, you don't.
Love Bea buzzzzzzzzzzzzing Off, Over and Out of here now x
P.S. Stop that now!

Subject: Birth
Can't you B Good!
Yuck. Woke up this morning with a chocolate roll stuck in
my eye and fake cream and jam squadged over my face.
Hasn't helped my complexion one bit! Still feel sick. Have
had to drink a pint of ginger beer to stop the sicky yicky
icky feeling. Wonder if this is how Mum feels when she
goes on about hangovers?

Of course I didn't snog (you old-fashioned romantic). It
was a midnight feast in our all-girl dorm to persuade Maya
to stay (and no, there was no lez action! I know your
mind). Her dad arrived this morning in his red Ferrari, to
whizz her home on his way back from something or other,
and she just waved him off. So at least it worked getting
Maya to stay.

Essay question – Should dads be allowed sports cars?
Aren't boyfriends meant to have sports cars, not old dads?
How embarrassing is it to have a dad drive around thinking
he's eighteen on red rollerskates, rather than pottering
along in a dull Volvo. Five hundred words by Monday.

It's still raining, like yesterday. Fully recovered from no

chocolate, but have big new spot the size of an elm tree sprouting on my chin, and I looky likey the wicked witch of the west. Can spots really be a result of chocolate? Think I will have to make myself a hot chocolate with marshmallows, if there's any left after last night. It was a hell of a non-leaving party, even without a snogathon!

Better go as I've sneaked out of artisticness to go to the loo, or rather to write this. Tomorrow, rain or pour, the hell of camping begins . . . We are being tipped into the wilderness to survive. If I do, I will write on my return.

Loving the Bea xxxx

Your pure white chocolate Lilybelle x

P.S. Outside the world is raining but inside the sun shines baby!

And talking about jeans (you can't spell!), my new jeans are ACTUALLY better than yours – official!

Actually

The party last night was damned fun. We played double truth or dare, strip poker and a game where you wrote on each others backs with chocolate fingers. The person with the back had to guess what was being written on them otherwise they didn't get the chocolate.

We also invented the Ministry of Silly Dancing and Dressing. All clothes had to be worn inside out and back to front, or upside down. This is a very good way of having fun. Of course, it woke Ann up because Izzy couldn't stop squealing. We put so much make-up on that when Ann, witch woman, came in and told us to quieten down and turn the lights out, she shrieked in horror, which of course woke the other rooms and everyone invaded our dorm for a pillow fight. By then we had hardly any clothes on, and all the boys were there. Then Ann got the Prof, who came and broke it up. Maya said that it's proof of a good party if it has to be broken up, although preferably by the police. I'm not so sure – sounds like a bad movie to me. I think it was a good party because Maya decided to stay and that was the whole point.

Re: Birth

Dear Lily,

Not interested in your tales of orgies until I have one of my own. Saw the boy again in the ice-cream store. Grandma is not being helpful. She said if I baked him some cookies I could go and give them to him and then I'd have a reason to talk to him. He may be cute but not that cute! Any cookies I make, I'm eating.

Meanwhile, depressed that Gramps has a red sports car. Does your theory count if applied to grandfathers? Is it worse? Thought so. Driving into New York (where buffest boys come from) for a few days of studying the art of shopping. Am thinking of swapping parents for grandparents permanently.

Happy Camping.

B x

Show Me the Way to Go Home — The Camping Highlights

Being bunged into an army lorry at dawn was one of the nice bits of camping. The sunrise was all pink, orange and puddingy. The birds were just beginning to sing, and the air had that smell of clean damp earth. The one thing that CampHappy was beginning to teach me was how I appreciate the early mornings. Occasionally.

All that feeling of contentedness soon disappeared completely – I punched Izzy in the face (by mistake – she walked into the space I was stretching into). The others say I did it on purpose. Maya is my only friend but she's been put into a different camp and wasn't there to defend me, while I'm camping with Izzy, Belle, William and Blake. Why is life so horrid? *Pourquoi?* Izzy is a downright tart, making eyes at William *and* Blake. Greedy, greedy girl. I know the boys are not mine, but honestly . . .

We had to make a camp – in the middle of nowhere – put up our own tents and cook round a campfire that we also had to build. Sounds so easy, but even the tent bit wasn't. Someone should have invented something that blows up by itself when you push a button, rather than having to hammer metal sticks in the ground like a caveman. Far more useful than going off to Mars or the moon. Inventors should concentrate on making camping work on Earth first, before trying to camp on other planets. They say it's to make us self-sufficient, but God knows why we need to be that? I prefer to think of it as communing with nature.

This is taken too far when they made us dig a hole in the ground to use as a loo. Pooing into a sewage pit isn't as fun as it sounds. Peeing in the lake is more hygienic. I have swum a lot.

There was no electricity, so every time you wanted a cup of tea you had to build a fire, and though nobody else wanted a cup when you asked (at least, not enough to help collect the firewood), they did once you'd boiled the kettle. It's strange how quickly drinking plain water seems fine. We were expected to fish for food and clean out their guts, liver, bacon, heart and everything yucky. And as if all that wasn't bad enough, after supper we had to sing songs around the campfire, taking it in turns to humiliate ourselves with the embarrassment of our singing, standing there in front of everyone like in assembly.

And there was no telly. And getting dressed inside a small tent is not funny.

The first night, Izzy got up to sing. Her singing, I had to admit, was good, too good. William and Blake went all gooey-eyed. Boys looking soppy at someone else lose all their buff. I don't like either of them.

I felt I just had to be the best at just about everything else we did after Izzy and her singing. It seemed like she'd set me a challenge.

I came first climbing up the mountain, built the fire every morning, dug a new loo every day and cooked the food. I became queen of cooking fried eggs, sausages, bacon, tomato and beans. Izzy pretended to be special, because she is a veggie-no-meat and she can't eat dairy products. No milk, yogurt, cheese, ice cream or butter – what does it leave? A couple of berries and a carrot. It's amazing she's stayed alive so long.

Izzy's so special, blonde and pretty, but everyone loves her for being utterly useless, demanding and tiny. It means they can all feel good because they helped her open a tin of lentil soup. True – she can't use a tin opener because of course, she's left-handed! She is the sort of girl that gives being a girl a bad name.

I was busy being team leader Wonder Woman (all I need is a cape and a tiara), when we were split up into groups for some night-time orienteering – in other words, a night-time stagger around the woods.

I was given a map, large torch and compass by ClimbMeister, although I didn't have the heart to tell him I have no sense of direction. Bea, Poppy or Mum know and would have laughed themselves to death. There are famous stories that I never want to hear again about me and my misdirections. But, I thought, it's another challenge. How hard can it be, even if you've got a *petit* brain?

Very hard. In a dark wood, with hooting owls, badgers

and foxes running after you. The moon was hidden and there were strange cooing noises, and crunching underfoot. I knew something was following us. Trees can look very human in the dark, and as the branches rustled I started to think about tree spirits and horror films. Really bad combo. We spent hours, walking around in circles and crossing the same river again and again. It was the only thing I recognised as I got more lost and even more scared.

And because I made out I SO knew what I was doing, we were the only group without an adult. But Lily Queen of All the Woodland I was not. I was shining the torch in the direction of these ghostly white things in front of me when Izzy started saying that she was scared, and was I sure I knew where we were. 'Of course I am!' I said, as something swooped out of a tree – and that's when I almost died. It was an owl, but I realised that too late and started falling, sliding down the side of this huge chalk cliff. Blake caught me just in time. I couldn't help it. I cracked. Bursting into tears and blubbing like a baby.

Belle was really sweet. They all were. I love Blake for saving my life. Then William took over and Izzy, shock-horror, worked the compass. We lost, came last (Maya's team came first), BUT we didn't die. I didn't die.

There I was, weeping apologies, but they all said not to worry, that I was good at other stuff and so funny when I was trying to be organised (slightly confused about this as feel I am v. sensible and v. organised) and that being a team and working together was good.

The next day we had to do some army-training-climbing-team-building stuff, which involved a lot of rope and walls.

It kinda got better after that. William was really lovely and gave me a piggy-back, when on the last day, I twisted my ankle swimming. I slipped on a fish in the mud while getting out. Hardly my fault. I never thought I'd say it but getting back to the comfort of CampHappy was near bliss. I couldn't wait to write to Bea and tell her my edited version. I could save up the gory truth of it all for when we saw each other.

Subject: Hell

Dear Wish you could Bea here,
How can I explain the past four days? Ah yes. Nightmare.

I'm not sure how I survived, but God must have a purpose for me. I know it wasn't forty days and forty nights, and I am not belittling Christ's achievement in the desert, but this was a Lily equivalent. And they gave me a map, which was of no help at all and I practically died.

I don't know who *j'aime* best, William or Blake. Suspect you've snogged most of Boston and New York by now. Can you be arrested for under-age *bisous* in the States?

News item: WARNING! There is a serial snogging British girl on the loose, hungry for mouth-to-mouth action. Lock up your sons. US males between the ages of twelve and one hundred are not safe. I repeat, NOT SAFE. She goes by the name of Bea.

There's archery on the lawn this afternoon. Will try not to pierce too many hearts but can't promise a thing. Am still trying to be good.

Lots of love,

Lily xxxxx

Subject: Everything Fine

Dear Mum,

Everything is fine, don't worry about my ankle as almost better and am still alive. It was nice to talk to you and Pops last night on the phone. Bay was so sleepy and sweet for a monster. I miss him too. I'm having a good time, made some fun friends and done some mad things, but I miss your hot Mars bar sauce over ice cream.

Hope your painting is making you happy.

Please don't tell Dad about my near-death camp disaster.

Lots of love,

Lily xxxxx

Subject: HA HA HA

Oh Lily,

How hilarious that anybody gave you a map and expected you to be able to find your way – like, anywhere. Did you tell them about getting lost going to the corner shop and the police bringing you home?

Or the time in Battersea Park . . . Or the time you were

on your rollerblades . . . Too many times. They should give you a free directional guide dog for the sighted.

Good news: fishman argh hasn't been here for two whole days. Mum has stopped cleaning and cooking. She was a bit freaked about the phone calls from camp about your ankle, but I told her you've got another one. I managed to stop her from calling Dad. Then the nightmare would have begun. Anyway she's as fine as she can be.
C U soon, crazy . . .
Love,
The Popsicle x
P.S. Saw Dad. Remind me never to go off with an old man like Dad. Even felt sorry for Suzi for one second, he's so grumpy and cross all the time.

Subject: Fast
Pops,
Thanks for everything with Mum. No time to chat. Glad Dad wasn't told. Nobody was hurt and bloody hell, Prof calling me now.
Lily xxxxx

Meditate on This

'I know – before you say anything, I know I was wrong and I've said sorry to everyone. And now it's all lovely,' I told the Prof, and smiled.

'I understand that, Lily, but if you sweep mistakes under the rug and do not look at why you make them,

116

you don't learn. There is nothing wrong with making mistakes – it's good, a necessary part of life – as long as you are willing to learn from them.'

I was lying on the sofa, which looked suspiciously like a psychiatrist's couch, feeling a little resigned. I hated admitting I was wrong. I knew what I had done was wrong, wasn't that enough? I wished I could have gone to hide, but there wasn't much chance with the Prof giving me his mad, beady stare, through those gold-rimmed specs. Who had advised him to buy those glasses? Did he have a wife hidden away who had said, 'Darling they're perfect, you look beautiful!' Or did he get a 2 for 1 deal?

Maya had already been given the forty-degree interrogation earlier on, because she was too pleased at winning the orienteering. The Prof said that she was too competitive. 'Have you met my Dad?' was her reply.

Unfortunately, that was the final straw for Maya. The end of the line, she said. 'Once small men with beards think they can start psychoanalysing me, sorry Lily, but it's time to go home.'

'Lily!' the Prof's voice shocked me back to the present. 'I'm going to ask you again. Why did you say that you could map-read? What made you lie so dangerously?'

'I didn't lie, I thought I could. I don't know . . . Look in the end, nothing happened.'

'But it could have.'

'I know I was stupid. My angel was looking after us, so it didn't.'

'You believe you have a guardian angel?'

'Of course.' My mother had always told me that I had one. Many of her theories were bonkers, but the angel thing I have always believed. 'Look, I told William and Izzy, so they took over. Why do I always have to be the one in trouble?'

'Ask your angel this: Why do you always have to be the centre of attention? Lily, I'd like you to meditate on that. Being in a team and living with other people is all about trust. That is why we do the rock climbing – not so Lily can get there first, but so everyone can have a chance to succeed. That's what climbing is about, teamwork and helping each other. Think about it, Lily. Will you?'

'OK,' I said reluctantly.

'You can go now. I don't want you to miss your lunch.'

I didn't want to miss my lunch either. We were having a picnic on the lawn before Maya left.

As I hopped away on my good leg through the back hall and out through the building, I did think about climbing and teamwork for about five seconds. Of course the Prof was right, I knew that, but there are exceptions. Social climbing, for example. That wasn't about teamwork and helping others. Why did I never think of these things at the time? After an awful lot of hopping, I made it out onto the lawn. The sun was out with a cool breeze, and I felt happy.

'Hey, there you are, Lily. I saved you some food.' Maya waved at me. Blake grinned madly and I smiled back.

'How come you're limping with the other foot now?' Blake laughed.

'Oh – am I? Hey, it must be better. Catch.' I threw my crutch at Blake, but sadly it hit William's head. 'I'm so sorry, William – shall I kiss it better?'

'No.'

'Oh, go on.' I chased him about the lawn and Maya helped me to pin him down, so he allowed me to kiss it better. Wonder if that means I've won the kissing competition with Bea? Suspect that peck on bonce under struggle might not qualify as *beaucoup de bisous*, but, hellzapoppin', how's Bea gonna know unless I tell her?

CHAPTER NINE

SADS

Ian and Blake bring down Maya's cases and say goodbye. I wait with Maya in the courtyard for Ann, who is driving her to the station.

'Now are you sure you don't want to change your mind and stay for the last five days?' I say, teasing her. I know it's too late.

'It's been fun, but I've had enough,' she says.

'You'll e-mail though,' I suggest.

'Of course, and we'll get together back in London. You'll have to come over and look at my parents one day.'

'Do they bite?'

'No, they are quite good, as long as you don't throw things at them.'

'You'll have to come and look at mine too. My family do bite, especially my little brother.'

'Maybe we can sign them into the zoo at Battersea Park,' she says with a glint in her eyes. We laugh. I know I have a new friend who isn't going to disappear, just because she's leaving. And the Prof said I didn't do trust; well, I do now!

I wave Maya goodbye and limp back to the Common Room. My leg might be better, but I convince JumpMeister that it's not quite well enough to do archery or croquet. Then I retire to watch the end of a fabulous afternoon film called *The Women*, all about bitchy 1930s Hollywood women stealing each other's husbands and gossiping, but in very glam dresses. Then I pick myself up, go back out, and join in the last of the croquet. I'm feeling better. Besides, what else is there to do but join in, now that I am an official team player?

The next morning I read Bea's latest e-mail.

Subject: OH MY yellow tricycle!
Dear Lilylice,
I am NOT AND NEVER HAVE BEEN a granddad snogger – let alone, great-granddad. Twelve to one hundred years old indeed? NO. I am officially mortally offended and you are hereby struck off The List. No more I Love Lily cards for you. No way baby. This is where you get yours! Biffboff!

But since I am stuck with you as best friend . . . It serves them right. Everyone knows you don't know your elbow from your knee, your right from your up, my nose from

your left. They must be dumbo-duh to give you a map.
Everyone knows that you think a map is a kind of wrapping
paper. Remember last year when you used your mum's
1970s map of India for my present – how cross was she?
You ruined her memories of being a hippy. Shame on you.

But what is really important is that I'm flying back
tomorrow. Just time enough to sleep off my jet lag and
then we can go to the top of Primrose Hill and roll down it
for fun. Remember when we did it last Christmas in the
snow and I thought your lips had turned blue with
frostbite, but you'd got some lurid bubblegum? Ha ha.
And no, I don't remember rolling in frozen dog poo.

Time to come home, not a boy in sight here. However, I
made friends with a local Labrador that I walk for a
neighbour who has hurt his back. I am the most Christian
person in world and God loves me. I don't think this counts
as bisous, but he's licked me several times (not the
neighbour, the dog) and always looks so pleased to see me. I
don't think it can really come to anything – you know how
odd families can be about breeding pedigrees. It sounds old
fashioned, but I'd set my heart on having babies rather than
puppies. I'll have to break it to him that I won't be able to be
faithful.

Less of the old dogs.

I think we should start a Society Against Dads and
Sports cars. SADS. Write letters to the prime minister, etc. I
think it's disgusting and they must be stopped. If only they
could see how SAD they look with no hair (have you

noticed that most men who're dads in sports cars are baldies?). Do they sell their hair to the devil in exchange for the red rollerskates machine? Does the prime minister have answers? Is the PM a SAD?

Would dads still do it if they realised how embarrassing they are? YES. My dad said, and I quote: 'I have been put on this earth to embarrass you. It is my job and I am willing to do it to the best of my ability. Which includes dancing at weddings, wearing sandals to show off my ugly feet, and clothes from the 90s.' A real SADS specimen.

He is sick. A tragedy waiting to happen and one day, his wife, my mother, will realise it. Then I can get a Suzi too. Does she have an ugly friend? He's not picky.

Oh, two boys? You is damned greedy. You must learn to share, but only with me.

Your dog-loving friend, woof woof.

Bea x (SADS chairwoman)

Subject: V. SAD

Dear Dogwoman,

You are sick and possibly should be reported to the RSPCA. You cannot marry a dog unless you are one. Are you? There have been comments at school . . . You have always been a champion wonder dog to me. I name you Bea, Best (Dog) in Show, bow wow.

Almost three days to go, then I'm home. I'm riding again this afternoon so I can get my bow-legged attractive cowboy walk perfected. Got to go clean out horse poo beforehand. Hmmm – don't you love animals? I swear, all you do is feed them and then they poo, a bit like Bay. In one end and out the other. At least Bay carries his own potty.

Have a good flight back and try not to snog the flight attendant, usually gay if male. They won't like dog licks.

Humans do it differently.

You green-eyed doggerel doggess. Bow WOW.

Lots of Lily-livered love xxx

I like talking rubbish with Bea because what is the point of discussing William and Blake with her when she doesn't know them? We'll have plenty of time to talk at home. But, in the meanwhile, I can write to Maya – she knows what I mean, even if she has deserted me. Both of the boys are now being so attentive to me that I can see Izzy quietly steaming with annoyance as they compete for my attention. I try not to be smug . . . I don't know what has changed to make things so different, but I am enjoying it.

Subject: Hi

Dear Maya,

How did Chelsea survive without you? You've only been gone a day and it's weird here without you. Wish you had stayed longer. I've learned to join in, be part of 'the team'. Prof is most proud. Have also learned that part of being in a team is that when Izzy says silly things you have to be like Thumper in Bambi: 'If you can't say something nice, don't say anything at all.'

I am biting my tongue. All matters of mouth make me
think of food. Yum yum, hope you are enjoying Peking
Duck with plum sauce in Chinese pancakes. I know I would
given the chance.

Can't make up my mind about Will or Blake. Can I have
them both? Geeky Ian is pining after you . . . It must have
been the way you hit him with your pillow. I think you like
him too? Admit it!
Got to run,
Lots of love,
Lily x

'Three days to go,' says Belle.

'I know, it's weird.' I reply – because I have learned you
have to say something, when somebody talks to you. You
can't just ignore them like I can with my family.

'The time has just vanished. One day we arrived, and
now we're just about to leave.'

'It's like rainbows,' adds Izzy. 'When they arrive and then
disappear. I mean, where do rainbows go to the rest of the
time?'

God was clearly testing me as we walked towards the
stable block.

'Actually, it's to do with light,' points out William.

Could I ever fall for a science geek? I could if he looks like
William, but then what about Blake? I am shredded, like a
secret document, with indecision. It's like being made to

choose between a chocolate nut sundae and a lemon sorbet. It's too cruel. I love them both. I can't choose. This makes me feel elated one moment and miserable the next. Maybe I'm not Lily but a see-saw. Being a see-saw might be easier, I think, until rudely interupted by the sight of a bald sausage dog on top of a very fluffy Pekinese in the stable yard. It is horrible and hilarious at the same time. I don't know whether to be sick or laugh. I am hypnotised by the ridiculous sight of the bald and the furry. What would their offspring look like?

'You perve, staring at those dogs,' is Blake's comment, but he walks over and stares next to me, along with Ian, Tony and Ben, until Jackie catches us.

'What are you lot staring at? Honestly! It's completely natural. Come on and saddle up the ponies.'

Natural? *Incroyable!*

How does one bald boy dog fall for a really hairy girl dog? And how can that be natural? It seems wrong, but when was love ever right? The amount of times you see short girls with giants, or short, fat, ugly old men with tall, beautiful, young models, is one of the many baffling things that I have to work out about how this universe plays jokes. Some of the universe's jokes are in bad taste. Do we have to end up with our opposite types? What is the opposite of me? I want to find a boy who will be just like me, but male obviously. Is that Blake or William? I know I pretend to like football to boys, but secretly I dream that I will meet a boy who doesn't like football either. Is that an impossibility? Will I have to lie my whole life about liking things I don't, like science or football, so I can fit in? Maybe. Boys always pretend they can do things when they can't, like dancing and cooking. Maybe all is equal in love and war.

I am thinking these very deep thoughts as we ride through the forest, up and around Lake Coniston. The sky is huge and blue and dotted with the cotton wool of drifting clouds, but it doesn't rain. The sun reflects on the huge lake and shimmers off its darkness in ripples of silver and black. It looks like a piece of crumpled-up tinfoil that you try to smooth out in the palm of your hand after you've eaten your sandwich. Each time the wind blows, it shakes the pretty blue and white boats moored around its edges. Lolly and I ride so well together it's as though we are one, in total harmony, though I am not as interested in eating grass as he is. Lolly is seriously making me consider Horse Whispering as a definite career option. But I can't think about a career right now – I still haven't worked out what to wear to the disco on the last night. Growing up and maturity is all about prioritising; the Prof told me so. But how do I prioritise between William and Blake? I am feeling sick with indecision. Who planted the Magimix in my guts?

Subject: Home Sweet Home

Dear Lily,

Have just finished my third duck and twentieth pancake. Must now eat three tubs of Cookie Dough ice cream – it would be rude not to. It was very fun meeting you too. I know we will still be friends even if you do snog William and Blake, but try not to do it at the same time. What are you wearing to the disco? Has stupid Izzy done anything stupid? Almost wish I'd stayed except for having my bedroom back. It's bliss. Dad fitted a plasma TV screen in it for me while I was away and I'm watching all my *Addams Family* favourites. *Très* cool, as you would so uncoolly say.

Have fun and don't die,

Maya

The Last Picture Show

'I'm sorry, but they've sent us the wrong film. Terribly sorry. We have no choice. It was supposed to be *Star Wars* but they've sent us *Chitty Chitty Bang Bang* instead,' Ann announces.

A groan goes up from the canteen, all except Izzy who goes, 'Hurrah!' The girl is too weird.

'Now, whoever wants to watch it can, otherwise I'm afraid it's whatever's on TV. There's a debate on education you might be quite interested in,' she suggests.

Where does Ann get her ideas from? Why would any child be interested in education? I say nothing because

128

saying nothing and smiling gets you into less trouble. I might look like an idiot, but I won't be told off for it.

How Fat Is an Elephant?

As soon as Ann disappears I come up with an excellent alternative. 'I know, why don't we escape from prison and invade the local cinema instead?'

'What's on?' says Belle.

'What difference does it make? I'm more interested in the journey than the destination,' I reply.

'I'm not sure,' says William.

'Come on, it'll be an adventure.' Trying to evoke some fun is like pushing the fattest elephant in the world, uphill. Not much fun.

'Haven't you had enough adventure?' asks Belle.

'Life is an adventure. Are you going to do the same thing for the rest of your life until drip, drop, plop, you're dead?' I say.

'Well, I . . .' Blake starts.

'Exactly, Blake. You're going to come?' I know he will, just by the way he was looking at me – all shiny-eyed and waggy-tailed. But William stands there silent.

'Come on, William. Don't be a wuss,' Blake chides him.

'If it's rubbish we'll come back. At least come as far as the shop?' I say.

'I might get some fags – haven't had a smoke in weeks.

And a few pints and a couple of whiskies, while I'm about it.' Blake is good at making people laugh. As if he'd ever get served . . .

'Dream on. The most anyone would serve you is a non-alcoholic cider ice lolly, and a pack of chocolate cigarettes,' I tell him, before pleading with Will. 'Please come, William.' He smiles. Yes!

This Way to Freedom

The gates are shut! Sugar! Not that there is anything sweet about it. CampHappy is really like prison.

'Only one thing to do: we'll scale the walls. Like when they have to escape in war films,' says William.

'Do you want a leg up, little Lily?' Blake asks.

'OK, pot calling kettle black. You ain't so big,' I say, smiling at him as I stand on the cradle of his hands and reach to pull myself up.

'What the hell do you weigh?' he says, struggling to boost me up. Hardly the comment of a gentleman. I glower down at him from on high.

'I don't think this is right,' Izzy squeaks.

'It's not left either,' I say, swinging my leg over the gate and disappearing with a thump down the other side.

'I don't want to get caught,' Belle chimes in.

'I like *Chitty Chitty Bang Bang*,' wails Izzy. Oh Izzy. Sometimes I can't help but cringe for the girl.

'Well bug off, wimps, we're going,' Blake adds. 'And don't say a thing.'

'Sure.'

Girls, honestly! Why do they have to be such, well, girlie, scaredy, micey things? And why do they always have to let down our sex by wimping out at the last moment? Well, not all girls – not Bea obviously, certainly not Maya or Poppy, but I have my suspicions that Suzi might have been like that. I wonder for a moment about Mum. No, not Mum. Mum's too solid.

What's worse is that some boys like girls to be like that. I decide that those boys aren't worth having if they don't appreciate the beautiful and brave. I think William and Blake do.

Once over the wall there's a thrill of freedom that goes through me, *un petit frisson*. I am a girl alone with the two best boys around and I am walking into town, bumping into each of them, laughing and joking. Blake tells one ridiculous joke after another. Boys always remember jokes – why don't girls ever? This is his best one:

A mosquito walks into a bar. The barman says, 'What would you like, Sir?'

'Water,' the mosquito replies.

'Still or sparkling?'

'Stagnant.'

Now is that worth remembering? So why do I?

We stop at the shop to buy some sweets, and Blake persuades William to buy him some cigarettes. When he's asked for ID, he pretends he didn't really want them but was testing the man for a school project. We make our escape, running out of the shop laughing with our lemonade and sweets.

We get into town. The cinema looks so old, with its peeling paint, that I think it's not open, but it's an old cinema club. Blake pays for us.

None of us had heard of the film, *Jules et Jim*, but I have my suspicions it might just be French, which is excellent. Blake and William ask the cinema girl if there is any kung fu in it. I pretend I'm not with them. I hope the film's set in Paris with girls wearing lots of black eyeliner and polo-neck jumpers, looking existential (not quite sure how you do that, but it sounds good), and boys with sultry dark eyes who drink coffee.

Inside the cinema we sit in the front row, with me sitting between William and Blake, as happy as a purring cat. It's a strange film set before the First World War – very black and white. But I can't quite believe that in the olden days they would jump in and out of bed with each other quite so rampantly! My great-great-grandmother would not have done that – I've seen photos of her. Basically, the film is about these two men who share – I know it sounds weird, but they share this woman whom they are both in love with, and she plays them for fools and never makes herself any happier. (I don't know why not – being with two boys seems a very good idea to me.) Then she kills Jules, the French one (Jim is the German one) and herself by driving into the sea. A nice romantic comedy with a happy ending – not!

I try to be as sophisticated as I can, but have to close my eyes from embarrassment with Blake sniggering in my ear each time sex is mentioned. Poor William gets so embarrassed at the bed scenes that he goes off to the loo halfway through, for ages.

AND

Alone with me now, Blake takes my hand and starts to breathe on the side of my face (luckily my spot has gone down). As I feel him moving towards me, I turn to him and, the next moment, he's slobbering into my eye! He was probably going for my mouth, but I turned my head, butting him in the nose, and he kisses me on my eyeball. Being kissed in the eye is as horrible as it sounds. Blake's subsequent 'Ouch!' makes it clear he doesn't enjoy my head-butt either.

We exchange whispered 'sorrys' before William returns, but Blake reaches over to hold my hand, squeezing my fingers together so hard I have to bite my tongue and pull my hand away. Is he being affectionate? It's hard to tell with boys because what they think is funny is often painful, like

Chinese burns. Hells bells, *Jules et Jim* have nothing on the complications of real boys!

THEN

There are no street lamps as we walk home, just the darkening sky, full of stars as bright as Christmas-tree decorations. I am desperately trying to talk about the film without mentioning that one girl has been doing it with two boys, when Blake disappears for a pee.

'What was that all about?' William asks. I don't know if he means Blake and me, or the film.

'Well . . .' I manage to get in, before he grabs my head with a vice-like grip, a bit like in the film, and kisses me. He opens his mouth so wide he covers both my mouth and nose with his huge lips. It's like wearing an oxygen mask, but without the oxygen, and I can't breathe. I don't know how long I can last before I pass out, but I push away just in time.

'I've been wanting to do that for the last two weeks,' he says, as if he's just conquered the North Pole. 'You didn't mind did you? I mean it wasn't too awful was it? I didn't hurt you?'

'No, it was fine,' I say, trying to recover my breath, while thinking that I'm not sure how much I like kissing. Why is there all this fuss about snogging? Is it something I could ever get used to?

'Fine?' he asks, bringing me back to the moment.

134

'Nice. It was nice, William. OK?' I try and pacify him by tip-toeing to kiss him on the side of the cheek. We turn to continue walking back and notice we are one person short. 'Blake, are you all right?' I shout.

'I'm here,' he says, jumping on top of both of us commando style and toppling me to the floor. Ha ha ha – apart from the bruised bottom I get. It is the perfect end to a perfect night.

Amazingly, Izzy has kept her mouth shut and we creep in the back just as Chitty flies off into the sky.

In bed I mull things over. What the hell am I going to do on the last night at the disco? Who am I supposed to have the last dance with, let alone figure out how I'm going to face them tomorrow morning over breakfast. Did Blake see the William kiss? Had William seen the Blake kiss? Do boys talk about things, apart from football, to each other? Why am I worrying about the disco, when I might not make it through breakfast? I'm not even sure I want to kiss either of them again.

At least I have won the *bisous*-ing snogging crown from Bea. She might be thinner, prettier, cleverer, and all those other -er things than me, but she only got a mongrel's kiss this summer, whereas I had two human boys! But if that is how humans really do kiss, I'm going to have to learn how to breathe through my ears or the top of my head, or somewhere else entirely.

CHAPTER 10

The Last Supper

Subject: Servants

Dear Maya,

Glad to hear you have the servants (parents) properly trained re installing TV. Sometimes they can get v. lazy when one is away. And you have a Nanny Meg? Oh, how the rich live. Bet you wished you were here for this last full day of activity. We did a pointless climb with ClimbMeister up a mountain to look at the view. We could have taken a helicopter or, even cheaper, bought a postcard. Now I am as hot and smelly as can be. Don't know if this is the reason that William and Blake aren't talking to me or the fact that I did the snog-deed with both of them yesterday. I must be a very bad kisser. Think I will go and hide in the lake and eat dragonflies. Can't be worse than the canteen food. *Bonne idée*, as we say in France!

Love,

The Water-Lily.

That was pretty much it for our last day of activities. *Très, très ennuyeux. Plus ça change.* After a nutritious picnic of wilting salad and sweating cheese sandwiches, we descended the mountain. OK, it was actually a very big hill, but the backs of my legs made me feel like it was a mountain, and it was so hot you could see the air shimmering in waves. ClimbMeister suggested we all go down to the lake for a swim to cool off. I lay on my back, floating in the water, feeling very alone but almost peaceful, until Blake ran screaming off the jetty to water-bomb me. After his hand-holding-eye-snog, I see this as an act of love and devotion. Neither William nor Blake talked to me all day. It was as though none of the snogging had happened, and I start to think that maybe my mind was playing tricks. It wasn't like I could ask them to make sure – imagine if I *had* made it up, how embarrassing the whole thing would be!

Gaggling & Giggling

We are going home tomorrow and we have to pack everything up from the dormitories. We also have to dress for the disco tonight, but all I want to do is lie in the bath and submerge myself. I can't tell either Belle or Izzy why. What am I meant to do? Have I mucked things up with both Blake and William? If so, how can I go to the disco? I will have to pretend that everything is fine, just like

Mum and Dad did when they were always screaming at each other. Talk will break the ice with the girls; I can do talking. 'Of course, borrow my mascara, lip-gloss . . . Did I mention the film was a *ménage à trois* – *très français . . .*' I know I'm blathering.

Belle and Izzy look up at me bewildered.

'You know, very French,' I say. Before long, we are like a bunch of geese, all talking, doing our make-up and trying clothes on all at once – a real gaggle of girls, I think, as Rosie and Fiona from next door squeeze into our room and join in.

'Do you think we'll ever see each other again?' Rosie says.

'Sure. Now shall I wear my skirt or jeans?' Izzy asks, wiggling her bottom, holding the items up.

'This top, or that shirt?' asks Belle. We are too obsessed with appearance to worry about the future.

'Which shoes? Which shoes?' I say, panicking.

These are real, major, life-changing decisions. Which shoes I wear seemed to make or break if I can go to the disco or snog anyone at the end of it. Let alone maybe two, and two whom I can't decide between, even if either ever speaks to me again. And would I survive being snogged by William again, with such a high risk of suffocation?

Maybe it's me that is so awful at kissing – does that

138

mean they are too embarrassed to look at me? This sudden thought has me terrified. I know it must be true. Suddenly shoes mean nothing compared to my inability to kiss.

'Come on, let's go down, Lily,' Belle says.

'I can't,' I reply. I might be wearing my best tiny green skirt and halterneck, but I am frozen to the bed by the realisation that I, Lily Lovitt, don't know how to kiss.

'Why not, you look great,' she coaxes.

'You don't understand. I – can't – go.'

'Don't be silly. Everyone's invited, and I think there's going to be balloons, orangeade and smoochy dancing,' says Izzy.

The way Izzy describs the disco makes me feel even more depressed. All my reasons to go are evaporating.

'Come on, it's not like you to be shy. We'll go down together and it'll be just another disco. What about all your CDs? They'll probably need them,' points out Belle.

'You can take them. I'll stay here.'

'That's unfair. Last night, you, William and Blake called us wimps when we didn't join in. Look who's being the wimpy one now?'

'I can't go down because, because I . . . I . . . Look. I don't know how to kiss.' It had tumbled out. I was showing my true pathetic self.

Silence. 'What?' says Izzy.

'Don't be silly,' says Belle.

'Look, it's simple. Just get your hand like this – so it looks like a mouth.' Izzy shows me her fist with a small opening in it above her thumb. It doesn't look like any mouth I've seen, let alone one I'd wish to kiss. She then demonstrates the first kissing position – lips pouting, head to side. I'm glad to say she does this with her hand and mouth, not mine. 'See? It's easy. Anyway, who are you snogging? Can I bagsy William? We *are* both blond after all.' This is the kind of logic that girls with very blond hair use, and is quite beyond my understanding.

'Izzy, the reason I don't want to go downstairs is that William tried to kiss me last night, and, well . . . I didn't know what to do. I almost suffocated. Are they supposed to put their mouths over your nose and mouth?' There, I've said it.

'William! Yuck – no, of course not,' says Izzy. 'What've you been doing all these years? Haven't you had a boyfriend?'

'Well, no, but I'm only thirteen. There's a boy in my street I've liked for ages, but he's busy with Amanda the hamface from Year Ten.'

'God, I've had boyfriends since I was ten. So has Belle.'

'No I haven't, Izzy,' murmurs Belle.

'But you had a boyfriend called Tom – you told me all about him last Christmas,' says Izzy.

140

'No. I made it up.' We all turn to stare at Belle.

'You lied to me?' asks Izzy.

'Sort of. Only because you always make everyone feel so stupid for being inexperienced. You're always telling people what you've done,' Belle says.

'I don't. It's not any different. I mean, it's not that much to boast about. They're just boys, and it's only kissing.'

'So how many boyfriends have you had?' I ask Izzy.

There's a big silence before Izzy speaks again. She gets up to put more lip-gloss on in a 'it really doesn't matter' manner. 'Two, but one wasn't serious,' she says into the mirror.

And Belle looks at me and I look at her and we burst out laughing. Izzy, the experienced teacher of kissing, is as unworldly as us, almost. 'What, what?' says Izzy before she joins in laughing. Then we link arms and, with my CDs, skip downstairs.

What's Your Tongue Doing in My Mouth?

Oh dear. Poor Jackie, Gordon, Ann and the other leaders have made such an effort with the balloons, ribbons, coloured lights and disco effect, but the ancient rock music they've got playing is keeping all the boys in the Common Room playing pool or filling their faces with chocolate cake, and none of the girls from the other teams are around except Rosie and Fiona, whispering in a corner, as usual.

'Do you need some help with the music?' I ask Ann.

'No,' Ann says. 'I've got it covered.'

'But nobody's dancing,' I point out.

'They're shy. They'll soon warm up,' she says.

'If we put this CD on, everyone will get dancing,' I say, waving it in front of her.

'Why? Is it rude?'

'No. Look, just try it.' Ann reluctantly puts the CD on and within minutes everyone appears and the dancing begins. Belle is first on the floor with Izzy, doing some crazy dance, wiggling their bums like they just don't care.

Even the boys start to dance. William keeps looking at me from behind the food table, shy and mysterious. But it's Blake who comes up and starts dancing with me, and it is Blake who remains there when the lights go down and the smoochy number starts to play. And it's Blake who puts his arms around me, says I look gorgeous and that I am the best girl in the whole of the camp. He says he'll miss me, and asks if I will write to him if he gives me his e-mail address. I feel guilty about William alone, staring at us. When I sneak a glance over Blake's shoulder, he's disappeared.

I wasn't sure I got the right boy before then, but Blake is the one who is here with me and has enough nerve to talk to me. We are dancing close, so close I can smell his deodorant. It isn't unpleasant. His hands are doing caterpillar moves up and down my back; it's comforting, like the way I stroke Bay if he's fallen down. I could almost fall asleep in his arms. That is, maybe, if we hadn't bumped into William doing mouth-to-mouth on Izzy. Honestly! He couldn't wait twenty-four hours before practising his oxygen mask technique on another girl. So much for mystery.

'Hey, watch where you're going mate!' Blake says. 'It's too hot. Shall we go and get something to drink, get some air?' he suggests, grinning like a hyena and doing odd things with his eyebrows. The heat is clearly getting to him.

Outside on the terrace, he pushes himself against me in the honeysuckle climbing up the wall. The moon is full and silver, painted onto the deep blue night sky. Blake begins kissing me, prising open my mouth with his and before I know it his tongue is in my mouth. It's very strange, but I go along with it. After a little while it begins to feel nice – no, better than that.

I now know why people like kissing. When you find someone you like kissing it's like the most delicious box of chocolates all to yourself *and* you don't feel sick afterwards. It's like riding on a brand new bike with the sun shining and the wind in your hair. It's like jumping in a puddle in wellington boots, or diving into the lake at Coniston. It makes you forget everything pointless, like time and space, or your parents shouting at you and sending you off to camp for three weeks, or heaven and hell.

Typically, I also forget I've got a cup of orange juice in my hand until it pours down Blake's back.

'What the . . .' he screams and jumps away.

'I'm sorry, I didn't . . . my drink . . .' He looks at me, shaking his head, and we both laugh. 'I'm really sorry.'

'Look, stop saying sorry. It doesn't matter, that's why we invented washing machines and soap.'

'Gosh, did you really invent all those things?'

'Ssh, come here. Now where were we?'

CHAPTER ELEVEN

Inside Out and Back to Front

My last night at CampHappy I sleep like a baby. In the morning I wake up early and energetic – being kissed gorgeously by a funny boy whom I never have to apologise to, because 'that's why washing machines were invented'. It's better than any sleeping pill. Is love never having to say sorry?

How cruel life is. Has it brought us together only to tear us apart? I will have to concentrate on absence making his heart grow fonder.

I go downstairs to use the computer, intending to write Blake an e-mail that he can look at as soon as he gets back home. I have used my super-powerful brain to memorise his e-mail address – SuperBlake@veryhotmail.co.uk. Brains are such excellent things. In fact, most things in life are just really good. What to write, though?

Subject: ME
Dear Super Blake,
I enjoyed being with you in the high security wing of
CampHappy.
Lots of love,
Wonder Woman (Lily)

Rubbish! I couldn't send that. I could try not being so clever and say:

Welcome Home Blake, love Lily X

Not exactly funny, though.

'You are up early,' says the Prof from behind me, giving me a fright. 'Are you packed and ready to go?'

It is the first time I've heard him sound happy. I suppose it's because we're all leaving. I nod in reply.

'Have you had a good time, Lily? Are you happy to be going home?' he asks.

'Yes, thanks. It's been surprisingly fun here. I've made some really nice friends. It wasn't quite as mad as I imagined.'

'How had you imagined CampHappy would be after reading our brochure?'

'Oh, you know, like a prison or mental hospital. It was more fun than that,' I tell him.

He walks away with his more familiar look of annoyance.

What had I said? I went to check any last minute e-mail emergencies before I continued to compose the perfect e-mail to Blake.

RE: Can't wait for you to get home
Dear Lil,
Can't wait for you to get home. So many things have changed. Bay has given up his potty. Mum has given up the fishman, who hasn't been about for a week. (Daren't ask where he is in case he reappears. Ignore things and they go away.)

She's madly painting, in the good sense, and she even remembers to shop but not always to cook. So I have been cooking some very passable omelettes *al formaggio, poulet à la* garlic and baked potatoes *à la* tuna fish. As you can tell, I'm almost as fluent as you. Call me Nigella or Jamie, whichever you prefer.

I have done all my college work and have no one to argue with. Doing loads of shifts at the café so I'm as rich as a queen. So I won't mind you coming home, and I might even take you shopping . . . Plus, how can I read your diary if you're away? So selfish.
Love,
Your big sis xxx
P.S. Billy and Amanda have split up. No more spam sandwiches.

It hits me then: In three weeks, I, who always keep a diary (professional dia-rhoeist), have written nothing. I still have a whole clean notebook that Suzi gave me. I decide it can be my new diary for the start of the school year. The important thing, I think, is that all is well with my world . . . that is, until I read the next e-mail.

Subject: NONE
Darling Lily,
I know you'll be a little upset, but Suzi and I are no longer together. She still wants to be friends with you, and I would be very happy if you wanted to see her. However, we are no longer living in the same place and I'm not sure where she is, but I'm sure she'll get in touch soon. Anyway, I hope you enjoyed your time away. Give me a ring when you get back and I'll take you, Poppy and Bay out for lunchypoos or some little treat.
Love, Dad

Blow me down. Changes? These are almost cataclysmic! No FishMan, no potty and now no Suzi. How much change can one girl take in twenty-four hours? Surely just getting a boyfriend is enough. If Mum and Dad split up, then Suzi and Dad split up – and she was really nice – what chance do I have with Blake, let alone with him living in Norfolk and me in London? What chance does Dad have of ever getting a girlfriend again? He might not be one of the saddest SADS, but did he lose Suzi because of this condition? Can any relationship work? Or was it just because Dad is old and angry? Poor Dad! And would Mum ever find someone nice? It seems like as soon as you get used to something, it changes. My head feels like a whirlpool of confusion.

The gong goes for breakfast and then I realise my T-shirt is inside out and back to front. I start to change it around. It's the Trucker Girl one, the T-shirt Suzi gave me . . . I am contemplating the cruelty of life, whilst getting stuck struggling with my T-shirt, when Blake appears.

'Oh, here you are, gorgeous. Wow! Do you need some help taking that off? Or do you want to show me your bra? Joke,' he says, with the cheekiest grin.

'No, I don't, thank you,' I reply.

'So, why are you getting dressed downstairs?'

'Oh, because it was dark when I got dressed. I put my T-shirt on the wrong way round and I've just found out that my dad's split up with his girlfriend. She gave me the T-shirt and, and it's . . . well, *tant pis!*'

'Bummer! *Tant* what?' And he puts his arms around me and kisses me better as we walk towards the canteen. 'What to have for breakfast? Remember, it might be the last horrible breakfast you'll ever have to eat. Pile it high – someone's got to fatten you up,' he says, smiling.

'I knew you'd cheer me up, Blake. Actually, it's no real change; my mum always burns everything until it's horrible, including breakfast. I'm not that hungry, anyway.'

Blake is busy piling everything on to his and my plates anyway, and carrying them to a table. I sit down. 'Hey, look on the bright side,' he says, pushing the humungous load of beans, egg, fried bread, sausages and bacon towards me. 'At least your mum will be happy.'

'How's that?'

'Surely,' he said, stuffing his mouth full of food, 'if your dad's got rid of his girlfriend, that'll make your mum happy. I know my mum was like murder until she forced my dad to give his girlfriend up.'

'What? No, silly. They're divorced. I shouldn't think it'll make any . . . Hang on, that would be weird – maybe they will get back together.' And will Mum want Dad back after Suzi? And do I want to live with Dad again?

'Anything's possible. Hey, would you come and stay with me in Norfolk at half-term? Say yes,' he asks, in a rushed way, eyes not quite making contact with mine.

'So, here are the lovebirds – kissy kissy?' teases Ian, coming over to us.

'Smoochy snoggerama?' says Izzy, as she, William, Belle, Tony and Ian laugh and crowd onto our table. I don't have a chance to say yes to Blake. Inside, I am smiling like a neon light, but I can feel my face turning the colour of tomato soup.

Time to Go

Ann is tooting the horn of the Land Rover, 'In you go, come along stragglers. Let's be having you.' She is still as odd as the first day. We push into the back, bags on our laps. Blake sits behind me and keeps tickling my neck and pretending he isn't, which is most annoying but v. sweet. When he denies it for the fifteenth time, I have no choice but to get my revenge. 'Blake, I wish I hadn't eaten so much at breakfast, I feel really sick.'

'Oh no you don't,' he says, seeing where this is heading.

'If I did, I wouldn't be able to help it,' I say, and start making vomiting noises.

'You are disgusting, Lily,' Belle says.

'Stop it, it's revolting.' Izzy shrieks.

Blake laughs, saying, 'You're sick, Lily, very sick.'

William looks appalled. Ian laughs.

I've always been rather pleased with my vomiting impression. Mum has suggested I could be an actress on the merits of it alone. '*Merci beaucoup, madames et monsieurs.*' I fake a little bow. 'Can't imagine where that came from.' I can't believe I've done it, not in front of Blake. And, he doesn't mind. I could never have done it in front of Billy. Ooh. Billy, I'd almost forgotten him . . .

Ann screechs the Land Rover to a halt. 'Is someone being sick in the back? Who is it? Out you get. Come on, the mess has got to be cleared up before we go any further.'

'But we'll miss our trains,' says Izzy.

'There isn't any mess,' I tell Ann.

'I don't care.'

'There isn't anything – come and look,' says Blake.

'I'm sorry, Ann, I was just being silly and playing a joke,' I say.

'Very funny. Now we're going to have to step on it if we're going to make your train,' she strops. 'If you miss this you're going to have to wait another two hours and it'll be all your fault.'

William looks at Blake and Ian, and then they look at me, and I look at Izzy and Belle until we all explode in giggles. It isn't funny, but we can't help it.

Ann sighs. 'Sometimes I don't know what's wrong with you children, really I don't,' she says grumpily, but it only makes us laugh louder.

His Lips, My Lips

At the station I run for my train. Blake carries my bag for me and kisses me just before the doors close and the whistle blows. I will always remember the way his lips pressed into mine, the smell of his piney aftershave and his cheeky grin. 'I'll write to you, don't forget to ask your mum about half-term,' I can hear him say through the window. I smile at him and nod.

I settle into my seat, opposite Izzy and Belle who are

152

on my train for part of the way home.

'So. You and Blake at half-term, eh?' says Belle.

'I don't know. Anyway, you can talk. What about you and Ian,' I say to her, 'and you and William?' I ask Izzy.

'I did nothing with Ian. We just talked. I like him,' Belle says.

'William!' Izzy snorts. 'Well, my boyfriend Lloyd won't like it.'

'I'm sure he wouldn't,' I murmur.

'So, where are you going in half-term? A dirty weekend in Paris?' asks Belle.

'Ha ha. Norfolk. Blake lives in a big house in Norfolk. He said his parents live on this estate called Blakensold. Sounds dire. Do you think it's a council estate?'

'Are you joking, Lily?' says Belle.

'Er, no.'

'You've never heard of Blakensold?' asks Izzy.

'No,' I mumble.

'It's like a really old stately home,' says Belle.

'Does he go to Eton or Harrow?' asks Izzy.

'I don't know. I didn't ask him.'

'Lord Bonner, that's it. That must be Blake's dad. He's famous for collecting sports cars,' says Izzy.

'What?' This is a bit much for me to absorb. It's crazy, Blake isn't that posh. I'm hypnotised by the cows in the fields rushing past. I can hear Izzy and Belle chatting, but

I'm lost in my head. My family might be mad, but I have a feeling Blake's might be just as bonkers.

'Hey, we have to get off here,' says Belle as the train slows down. 'Don't forget MSN messenger tomorrow and every night at six p.m.'

'Sure. Speak to you then,' I say, as if I'm seeing them later on.

On my own, I think about what they've said. Hearing about Blake and his family was so weird. How would we have anything in common? What would we do all day? Count his money or his cars? If I visit him, would he want me to help him spend it? Rich people should naturally feel guilty about having so much more. Maybe I could help with that guilt.

Blake is the type of boy that all girls dream about meeting. A prince among the frogs. This thought does not make me happy, though. If I've found a prince right at the beginning of my boyfriend life, I'll probably have to spend the rest of my days dating not even frogs, but probably toads or slugs. As I start to think about slugs they appear in my mind as sandwiches and I can imagine the taste. Why does everything turn into food in my head? Blake was right: I am sick, through and through. This is proven by the fact that I'm desperate to see Bea and Poppy, Bay and Mum, and even Dad. I can't wait to tell them about camp.

CHAPTER 12

Home Sweet Home

As the train draws into the station, I can see Mum holding Bay holding a placard that says: *We ♥ Lily*. The heart has little arms and legs protruding from the messy redness and a blue face on it. A Bay original, helped by Mum. I wave to them.

'Look at you!' are Mum's first words. 'Come here and give us a hug. You look like you've lost weight. Maybe I should go to camp.'

I hug her like it's been so long.

'I've been starving for you too, squadge,' I say, grabbing Bay. 'Let me give you a special raspberry cuddle.' I blow into his chubby neck until he screams with delight.

'Do you like my hair? Thought I'd have it done today,' says Mum.

'It's great. Makes you look loads younger. Hey, where's Pops?'

'Making you a surprise dinner. I'll carry your bag,' she says, picking up the luggage.

'Thanks. Wow, Poppy at the stove – is that wise?'

'She's picked up a few recipes in the café – she's pretty good. Oh Lily, it's good to see you. Did you have fun? Before I forget, someone called Maya phoned.'

'It was all right. Oh, OK, it was brilliant. Maya's my new friend from Chelsea, and a boy called Blake has asked a few of us to Norfolk at half-term. Theoretically could I go?' I say, crossing my fingers behind my back to stop it being an out-and-out lie.

'Theoretically, I don't see why not – if his parents . . . have they got enough space? What do they do?' she asks me.

Why do parents always want to know what your friends' parents do? 'I don't know, they're just rich. Thanks, Mum.' I kiss her cheek.

'Hey, what was that for?' she asks.

'Oh, just for you being you.'

'It's what I do best. Nobody can quite do me like me.' She seems in a *very* good mood.

'Hey, have you spoken to Dad recently,' I say, as we get in the car.

'No, I thought you didn't want me to. Why?'

'I got this weird e-mail from him today . . .'

'And?'

'Well, it said that he and Suzi have split up.'

'Oh! That's sad. I wonder why?' she muses.

'Dunno.'

'Oh dear. I suppose I should give him a ring. Put your seatbelt on.'

'Maybe we could ask him over for dinner, just to be kind, and . . . and I can tell him all about camp. We can have a nice family dinner with Dad back at home. He'd like that, wouldn't he?'

'Yes, I'm sure he would. Lily, why are you talking so strangely?'

'What have I said? Stop looking at me so suspiciously,' I tell her.

'I don't know what you're up to, but I'm sure it's something . . .'

'Mum, we're not even home yet and already you're accusing me.'

'Oh, I'm sorry, my Lil chick. You're right. I don't know what's wrong with me. Why should you be plotting anything?'

'Exactly. I'm just trying to be nice, isn't that right, Bay?' I say, hiding my face in his tummy. How do mums always know?

Potty on the Brain

It is great to be home back amongst the colour and the mess. Usually I don't even notice Mum's paintings, but I realise I have missed them. Everything is comfortingly the same – books still in piles on the floor, magazines scattered like cushions about the place. Nothing has really changed except for new dining room chairs. I give Poppy a quick hug in the kitchen while she cooks, then I take my bag upstairs to tidy myself up before dinner. I brush my hair until it looks like my face is coming out of a bush. It feels like I've been away for two minutes yet, in other ways, two months. I feel so different. I can't remember what I'd been so angry about, or why, before I went away, but it's nice not to feel so cross anymore. Poppy bounds up the stairs, bursting into my room.

'You look great, Lil.'

'So do you.'

'Do you like this?' She shows off a blue halterneck top with sequins splashed across it like a bolt of lightning. 'I bought it down Portobello Market on Saturday.'

'Yeah, can I borrow it?'

'Maybe. So?'

'So what?'

'Gossip? Something must have happened in three weeks away that you didn't tell me about.' Poppy lounges across my bed, whilst I unpack.

'Not really. No,' I say, remembering the waterfall, Blake, Maya, *Jules et Jim,* William, getting lost in the woods, sleeping in a tent, pillow fights, mountain climbs, Lolly, Blake's kisses on the last dance . . . 'Except, what about Dad? Suzi's left him.'

'Really? Are you sure? How come he told you and not me?'

'Don't know. He sent me an e-mail. He didn't tell Mum, either. Do you think they'll get back together?' I whisper, conspiratorially.

'Who? Dad and Suzi?'

'No! Mum and Dad, loonygoon.'

'Of course not, you ignoramus idiot. Dad left Mum because she's a lunatic. Not for Suzi. Why would he come home?'

'To be with us? Who wouldn't want to?'

'Oh, poor, simple Lil. Grown-ups are much too complicated to do what they want just because they like people. Anyway, they're divorced. It's never going to happen.'

'Miracles happen all the time,' I say.

'Strange things happen, but Mum and Dad are so not going to happen. Hey! Billy and Amanda split up.'

'When did they?'

'I wrote and told you.'

'I didn't take it in.'

'Last week. Now there's a chance for you.'

'I don't know, he's a bit old and a bit cheesy. There are better boys in the world.'

'And you've met one?'

'You know, I just might have,' I say. I couldn't stop myself smiling.

'So, what's his name?' she asks, jumping on me and tickling me.

'Blake! Help!' I say, but manage to escape.

'Blake help what? I want phone numbers, addresses, bank details. I'm not letting any old pauper pawing the royal Lilypad.'

'Yeah yeah, servant. Where's my dinner, I'm starving?'

'Servant? Who's calling who servant?' she yells, and chases me round the room until she catches me screeching and wriggling against the tyranny of her tickling. Poppy gets me every time – she sits on my tummy.

'Help, help,' I call, in case I should asphyxiate and Poppy is dragged away and hung in a gas chamber for my murder. I am selfless.

Mum shouts back. 'Turn it down, girls, or the neighbours will be calling the police again.'

The typical reply of the good Samaritan. I shout for help and she mentions the noise.

'Mum,' calls Poppy, 'Lily's got a boyfriend and she won't give me the details. It's not fair.'

Bay runs in with his old potty on his head and no

pants, jumping and screaming. He might have stopped using his potty but I am not convinced that wearing it as a hat is a great improvement. 'Oh, just tell her, Lily. Then we might have a chance of some food. Bay, shorts?' says Mum, peering at me from the doorway. 'So who is he? What do his parents do?'

'I don't know. Enough interrogation!' I know now I am home. Home, sweet home.

Buzzing Bea

'Bea? I'll be round in five minutes. I've got to go to the chip shop for everyone. Poppy tried to kill us with her Salmonella Special Chicken.'

'Lily? You're not on the phone are you? Thought you'd left already,' says Mum.

'It's only Bea. I'm going!' I shout back. 'See you in five.'

'Bea!'

'Lily!' We both scream. Scream and jump around in each others arms like long lost comrades from a past war. Where to start? What to catch up on first, I wonder, until I remember what's really important.

'I've won the snogging competition,' I announce. But we both say it at the same time.

'No, I have,' I reiterate.

'No, I have,' she insists.

'What's yours called?' Bea asks.

'Blake. I told you about the boys right at the beginning and it happened on the last dance, at the last night's disco . . .'

'Witness statements?'

'No, but . . .'

'I've won, then. I was caught on camera at the local fair, snogging a boy in a competition for charity.'

'That's unfair. That's engineered. It's cheating.'

'It's better than that, it was for charity.'

'Well, I suppose that beats love?'

'What are you saying? Don't tell me Lily's in lurve? No way, *José*! OK, who is he? I need details, fingerprints, bank balances . . .'

'Bea stop it, you're scaring me. You remind me of my family.'

'Your mum or Poppy?'

'A sickly mixture. Hey, we better get to the takeaway before Mum calls the police for her missing dinner.'

'OK, sorry. So tell me all about the Blake. Weird name,' she says.

'Look, there's a problem,' I tell her.

'What's wrong with him? Is he a crazed psycho?'

'No, it's worse than that. Much worse.'

'What's worse?'

'He's, well, he's rich. I mean really rich.'

'You must be a weirdo-seeking missile. Lily, are you crazoid? What is wrong with him being rich?'

'I don't know, but . . . they're not like us.'

'It's probably not his fault. What are you like? Can you listen to yourself? If you like him, you can get through this.' And she's laughing hysterically at me.

'I knew you'd laugh. But it's strange – he lives in a palace in Norfolk and he wants me to go and stay with him. He'll probably send a helicopter or a private Lear jet to pick me up. It'll be really embarrassing.' I look at Bea. I am getting no sympathy. 'Haddock and chips three times please,' I say to the chip man.

'If you want me to share your embarrassment, you only have to ask. As your best friend, I'm willing to come to Norfolk with you, as long as you give me a chip. Does he have a twin brother?'

'Don't know, but his dad collects sports cars. You might have a chance with him . . .'

'Eeeek, Lily! You mean my very own SAD?'

'I find you a boyfriend, and already, complaints. Bea, you of all people should know that love knows no boundaries. Remember the dog?'

'No wonder your parents sent you away. Freak. Give us a chip,' she says again.

'Are you forgetting your parents sent you away too?' I point out, as we head back to mine.

CHAPTER THIRTEEN (Too bad luck)

CHAPTER FOURTEEN
One Way to Tell It

The next day I call Maya. 'Hi Maya, it's me, Lily. How are you?'

'Hey, Lil. It's great to hear from you.'

'Do you want to meet up today?'

'Love to, but Dad's arranged a hideous family get-together. What happened in the end? Did you snog William?'

'No, not really . . . William, Blake and I escaped the loony bin for the night and went to the cinema in town. Belle and Izzy were being complete wimps and wouldn't come. William leaped on me all slobbery and I almost suffocated.'

'God!'

'I know. I mean, I couldn't make up my mind between Blake or William, but when it came to the last dance at the disco, Blake was there and William was snogging Izzy!'

'She always was after him. Remember her pretending to drown? So he had to give her the kiss of life?'

'And she's already got a boyfriend called Lloyd. But Belle and Ian were really sweet,' I tease.

'No! He was mine!' Maya jokes.

'Yup! Sorry. Hey, Blake was saying we could go and stay in his mansion in the country at half-term. Would you come?' I know he hadn't asked the others, but I couldn't go alone. I needed back-up, and that meant getting all my friends invited as well. Besides being less nerve-racking with his family, it would also be much more fun. And he does live in a big house.

'He hasn't asked me.'

'But if he did, would you? Just for a couple of days?'

'Sure. Look, my mum's yelling. I've got to go.'

'Try to do MSN messenger at six p.m. with everyone.'

'I'll try. Can you come round tomorrow? Come and see my new plasma screen.'

'Try keeping me away,' I tell her.

'I thought everyone would forget me. I'm glad you called. It's a bit depressing back home. Typical. Desperate to get back, and bored when I do.'

'Forget? How could we forget your father's ponytail when he came to pick you up in that red rollerskate!'

'Don't. I intend to cut it off when he's asleep. I'm

going to say Mum did it when she was drunk. Bye!'

This Maya girl is inspired!

Post-Camp Nerves

The longer I leave writing to Blake, the harder it becomes.
I really like him, but as another day passes, the whole
camp thing starts to feel like a dream. I'm not sure what
parts I have been making up in my head. Maybe I should
have done what Maya said she thought we'd do – forget
everyone/thing. Did I really snog Blake and cover him in
orange juice? Did he really ask me to go to Norfolk, or
had he asked everyone to go? I thought I was making it up
. . . And what would I say if I wrote to him? And why
should I have to write to him first – why wasn't he writing
to me? I knew the answer to that. I didn't remember to
give him my e-mail address before we said goodbye. It was
my fault. I had to deal with it.

Dear Blake, (Seemed too strange)
Hi Blake, it was so nice meeting you! (Wrong)
Yo Blake, you are one great smoocher . . . (So fake).

I tried to imagine what I would say to him if I called him
up. The point of e-mail is that it is like the phone, but
gives you a chance to be clever and funny. Help! Maybe I
am losing my sense of humour! Impossible. But having

to explain the point of e-mail to myself, maybe I am more like Dad than I want to admit. Would I too leave Mum for a young secretary and buy a sports car once I'd reached forty-eight?

Subject: Hello

This is so weird, Blake. Don't quite know what to say except that it was great meeting you and I had lots of fun with you – both wet and dry (how's the orange shirt?), indoors and outdoors.

Anyway, hurrah! Mum says it's fine for me to visit you at half-term. Just as long as your family aren't psychopaths or murderers. I said I thought it unlikely, but it's always safer to ask. Are they?

We're all going on MSN Messenger tonight at 6, if you get this message in time, or you can always call me at home (number below).

Love,

Lily xxxxx

P.S. I think you are a kisser *par excellence* (French for very good indeed!).

Then came the terrible moment afterwards when I realised sending it was an awful, hideously embarrassing mistake, but it was too late. It had gone.

What if . . . What if . . . What if . . . Those thoughts don't stop once they get on the Circle Line of your brain, round and round and round . . . until you end up

screaming, 'Poppy! Why have you stolen my lip-gloss?'
which has nothing to do with the reason why you need to
scream, but it'll do as an excuse – you can always find a
reason to scream at your sister. Well, I can.

'What? The lip-gloss on your mantelpiece? Dumbo,'
she says, coming into my room.

'Yes. Sorry. Oh, Poppy, my life is over. I've written this
e-mail to Blake and it's really soppy – I mean so soppy it's
dripping.'

'He'll love it.'

'But I think I imagined everything that happened
between us.'

'Oh well. Even if you did, at least you won't bump into
him at school or in Battersea Park. I mean, realistically,
how often do you go to Norfolk in a week?'

'Don't be so sensible. You just don't understand what
it's like to be me. I'm going to have to die.'

'No, you're right, I don't understand. I'm lucky that
way. And if you die I'm definitely having your lip-gloss,
and your jeans.'

'Sorry Poppy, I've bequeathed them to Bea.'

Six p.m. won't come fast enough.

MESSENGER

Dingbelle – Anyone here?

Mizzylzzy – Hi cuz.

LotsofLily – Is it girls only?
Blake567 – Lily, you get my mail?
MizzyIzzy – Is Will coming?
LotsofLily – Mail you right back.

Who wants to do chatroom when there's a special message just for you? I logged into my mail and I couldn't get to it fast enough.

Subject: YOU
Dear Lily,
Can't wait to see you again. You are GREAT and the best kisser in French, ever. Did you know French for kissing is *bisou*? Will call you later . . .
Love,
Blake x

C'est la vie! This is the life, my lovely life. I don't know if my French has improved, but my kissing certainly has. Somehow, when I wasn't looking, the summer just got a whole lot better. How does that happen?

The Lilicionary

Translations of some of my favourite French phrases (and my mum's least favourite):

absolument pas – absolutely not
alors – so
allez oop – there you go
amour – love
anglais – English
beaucoup de bisous – lots of kisses
bonne idée – good idea
bonne maman – good mother
café au lait – coffee with hot milk
c'est la vie – that's life
c'est trop ennuyeux – this is too boring
courage, mon ami – courage, my friend
croissant – buttery breakfast pastry
d'accord, très bien – OK, very good
dégueulasse – disgusting
délicieux – delicious
excusez-moi – excuse me
fantastique – fantastic
français – French
incroyable! – incredible!
intéressant – interesting
j'adore Paris – I adore Paris

j'aime . . . – I like . . .

j'arrive – I arrive

j'aime les berets – I love berets

je ne comprends pas – I don't understand (should use this more)

je ne suis pas amusée – I am not amused

je pense – I think (therefore I am)

je suis desolée – I am desolated/sorry

je suis formidable – I am terrific

je suis très fatiguée – I am very tired

je suis un rock star – I am a rock star

l'argent, Maya, n'est jamais ennuyeux – Money, Maya, is never boring

légumes – vegetables

ordinaire – ordinary, regular

Mademoiselle – Miss

magnifique – magnificent

ménage à trois – très français – relationship for three – very French

merci beaucoup, mesdames et messieurs – thank you very much, ladies and gentlemen

moi! – me!

ma chérie – my dear (*mon cher* if you're talking about a boy)

mon petit choufleur amour – my little cauliflower love (sounds better in French, like most things)

oui, oui – yes, yes

pain au chocolat – croissant with chocolate inside
pardon – sorry; pardon
par excellence – very good
petit – small
petit café – small café
petit déjeuner – breakfast
petit frisson – little shiver
pis allez – go away
plus ça change – so what's new?/nothing ever changes
poulet à la – chicken cooked in a particular way
pourquoi? – why?
quel dommage – what a shame/pity
quelle surprise – what a surprise
quelle horreur – what a fright/horror
tant pis! – too bad!
tarte au citron – lemon tart
tout l'amour est mort – all love is dead
tout les champignons – all of the mushrooms
très – very
très magnifique avec les marshmallows – very good with
  marshmallows
très rustique – very rustic/country
vive la France! – hooray for France!
voilà! – there!
vraiment – truly/really/very
zut alors! – oh my God!